CLOSE CALL!

Red Sox center fielder DT Green lunged, made a short hop grab of the liner, and came up firing in a single motion.

His arm propelled the ball forward like a cannon shot. The throw honed in on home plate like a cruise missile seeking its target. Boston's catcher Rick Waldman braced himself in front of the plate. The ball flew all the way to home on the fly and hit the catcher's glove at the same instant that the Yankees runner hit the catcher's leg. Waldman went down in a heap on top of the runner as a cloud of dust rose up around the play.

When the air settled the umpire saw the runner's leg, inches short of the plate, and Waldman's glove, with the ball still in it, resting on the Yankee's chest.

"You're outta here!" the ump screamed.

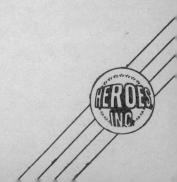

Other books in the ROOKIES series:

#1: PLAY BALL
#2: SQUEEZE PLAY
#3: SPRING TRAINING
#4: BIG-LEAGUE BREAK
#6: SERIES SHOWDOWN

Rookies
PLAY-OFF PRESSURE

Mark Freeman

BALLANTINE BOOKS ● NEW YORK

RLI: <u>VL: 6 & up</u>
IL: 6 & up

Copyright © 1989 by Jeffrey Weiss Group, Inc.

Produced by Jeffrey Weiss Group, Inc.
96 Morton Street
New York, New York 10014

Library of Congress Catalog Card Number: 89-90949

ISBN 0-345-35906-2

Manufactured in the United States of America

First Edition: September 1989
Second Printing: April 1990

To my parents . . . for taking me to and sitting through all those Little League baseball games when I was growing up

ONE

A cloud of dust choked the San Francisco Giant's runner as his hand searched out the bag after his headfirst slide. Blinded by the grit in his eyes, all he could do was listen as the umpire screamed out the verdict.

"You're outta here!"

Roberto Ramirez hopped off the pitcher's mound and raced toward the Dodgers' dugout. His teammates slapped him on the back and offered high-fives all around.

"Whayda go, Magic."

"Good pitching, Ramirez. We've got 'em now."

As he had been with the Los Angeles Dodgers for only a month, it still seemed strange to Roberto to be a member of a Major League team. It surprised him that he had been accepted so warmly and easily. It was a wonderful surprise.

Having left Rosemont High only a little more than a year ago, Roberto's rise to the top was meteoric. A rookie season with Salem in A ball went perfectly. A great spring training got him a shot in AAA at Albuquerque. And now, promoted to the big club: the Los Angeles Dodgers.

The fact that the Dodgers were on cruise control toward another Western Division title made for a lighthearted and carefree organization. Everyone was used to winning, expecting to win, and, in short, going to win. Roberto's success on the mound, three wins and no losses, made him a contributing member immediately.

"Two more innings, Ramirez," the Dodgers' pitching coach, Dave Westrum, said. "Then our magic number will be down to one."

The magic number was a reference to how many wins the Dodgers needed, or losses their challenger, Houston, needed, to give the title to L.A. With two weeks to go in the season, it was only a question of when it would happen.

The Dodgers already had a big 6-2 lead, and the laughter and joking on the bench was an early celebration of the expected victory. Roberto just had to finish it up.

Taking the mound in the eighth, Magic quickly got the first two batters out. In his haste to end the inning he grooved a fastball down the middle, and paid the price. Mac Wilson's home run cut the lead to 6-3.

When the Dodgers ended their half of the eighth without having scored, they went out to finish off the Astros and then wait for tomorrow's game to celebrate the clinching of the title. But, they forgot to tell the rest of the teams in their division.

Roberto walked the first batter in the ninth. The L.A. crowd seemed annoyed at the temporary delay.

"Put 'em over the plate, Ramirez," the fans yelled. "Let your teammates get 'em."

"Throw strikes, kid. Make 'em hit it. Make 'em hit it." Roberto tugged on his cap and tried to concentrate. "Strikes. Throw strikes!" he muttered.

His next pitch would have been a strike if the batter hadn't laced it into left field for a single. The runner on first rounded the bag but held at second. Suddenly, the 6-3 lead was looking shaky.

Steve Henderson, the burly catcher for the Dodgers, trotted out to the mound. With the additional weight of all the catcher's equipment, the 220-pound mass didn't break any speed records.

"Hey, Rook. What's going on out here?" he asked.

Roberto grabbed the bill of his hat and lifted it from his head. He wiped the sweat off his brow with the sleeve of his royal blue baseball undershirt.

"I just got a little careless, I guess," Roberto said, shrugging. "I'll bear down."

"Cripes, I hope so," Henderson groaned. "Let's get this game over with!"

Roberto leaned over and plucked the rosin bag from the ground as his battery mate headed back behind the plate. He felt like he'd just been politely chewed out for screwing up.

"Okay," he mumbled under his breath. "I'll give this next guy the heat and blow it by him."

Henderson had the same thought. Roberto looked in for the sign and saw one finger flashed, signal for the fastball. After checking the runners, Roberto wound up and threw. The ball bounced a foot in front of the plate.

"Geez, what was that?" Roberto said as he slapped himself on the leg. "I can't believe I threw that!"

The next sign was for a curve ball. Again, Roberto checked the base runners and went into his stretch. This time, his pitch sailed way wide of the plate. The count had quickly fallen to two and oh.

Tommy Lasorda, the Dodgers' manager, quickly jumped up from his dugout perch and ran out toward the mound. The look in his eye made Roberto cringe.

But when he arrived at his pitcher's side, Tommy was concerned but good-natured.

"You all right, Roberto?" he asked.

"I feel fine, Coach. Really. I think I was just overthrowing those last two pitches."

Lasorda looked at Henderson. "How about it? Is he okay?"

"Still got plenty of pop on those pitches. He's just a little wild," Henderson said, shrugging. "Tough call."

Lasorda almost reached for the ball in Roberto's glove, but at the last moment decided to stay with him. "Okay, kid. Keep it low now but throw some strikes."

Magic nodded. "You got it."

When everyone left the mound, Roberto felt his heart start pounding. His breathing became labored, and sweat poured off his forehead. He knew from the sick feeling in his stomach that he was having another attack of nerves.

Despite his brilliant pitching efforts, Roberto had been plagued off and on with a nagging doubt in the back of his mind — a doubt that someday, for some reason, he would lose it. He felt that the batters would catch on to him and he wouldn't be able to get anyone out. Those doubts were now, suddenly, in complete control of his mind.

Henderson squatted down behind the plate and started to give the sign. When he looked out at his pitcher he knew something was seriously wrong. He'd been briefed before Roberto joined the team that there was a potential problem. The coaches told him it wasn't anything serious and might not ever show up again. But the catcher now knew what they were talking about.

Roberto barely nodded when he looked down at his catcher. As he started his delivery his motion was so awkward and tentative that the throw nearly went sailing into the backstop. Only an athletic leap by Henderson saved it from being a wild pitch.

The Dodgers catcher took two steps toward the mound but the umpire stopped him. "I hope we're gonna play ball, Henderson. If you go out there again, you sure as hell better yank him."

Not wanting to make that decision on his own, the catcher retreated behind the plate. He glanced toward the dugout and caught Lasorda's eye. Roberto paced around the circular patch of dirt in the sea of green grass. His head was swimming. Desperately, he tried to pull himself together.

"Okay. Slow it down. Slow it down," he told himself as he took several deep breaths. He felt a black circle slowly close in around his field of vision. Placing his hands on his knees, he leaned over and tried to shake the fog from his mind.

The crowd noise finally broke into his consciousness. He stood up and turned to look at the massive scoreboard out in center field. He was stalling for time but trying not to look conspicuous.

"You've got to do it," Roberto said to himself over and over again. "You can get him out!"

Lasorda was just about to jump from the bench and head for the mound when Roberto turned and took his position on the rubber. He was still shaky, but he held himself together firmly while he looked for the sign.

Henderson signaled for a fastball. With his hand and glove pointing downward, he tried to tell Roberto to calm down. He wondered if anyone else could see what was happening.

Maybe he'll miss it, Roberto prayed as he started to throw.

The pitch wasn't a great one. It had pretty good speed and was over the plate, though, and when the batter let it go by Roberto sighed in relief. "Strike one," yelled the ump.

"Two more now . . . just like it," his teammates yelled.

"You can do it!"

Roberto chuckled, a fleeting moment of relief from his fears. "I hope they're right."

He waited for Henderson to call for another fastball. Nodding, he fired another pitch for the outside corner. This time the batter didn't let it go.

Roberto heard the crack of the bat and couldn't bring himself to turn and watch. He knew it was solid contact, and his shoulders slumped in worried anticipation. The crowd's gasp and sudden silence told him what he already knew.

"It's outta here," he grumbled to himself.

As he kicked the dirt and stuffed his glove onto his hip, Roberto suddenly heard the crowd explode in cheers. He spun around toward center field just in time to see Rickey Salazar sprawled out on the ground, but holding up his glove with the ball in it for everyone to see.

Elated, Roberto jumped up and swung his fist in the air. "All right!" he screamed.

As suddenly as the attack of nerves had hit, the old competitive fire in Roberto was reignited. Fiercely pacing the mound, he anxiously waited for the ball to be returned from the outfield. He pounded the ball into his glove and rushed to assume his position on the rubber.

Lasorda, Henderson, and the rest of the team immediately knew that the old Roberto was back.

"Okay, kid. Let 'em have it," Lasorda yelled from the dugout.

Henderson pounded his huge catcher's glove and set up behind the plate. "C'mon, Rook. You've got 'em now. Let's do it!"

Six pitches and six strikes later, the Giants were retired. With the victory, the Dodgers were within one game of clinching the Western Division title.

As he walked off the mound and headed for the dressing room, Roberto was mobbed by his teammates. They pounded him on the back and offered their congratulations.

"Good game, Ramirez."

"Whayda fire out there, kid."

"Looking good, Magic Man. Keep it up. Keep it up."

Roberto slapped high-fives with them all and laughed and joked back to the clubhouse. But when he finally had a moment alone in front of his locker he took one last huge sigh of relief.

He remembered the feeling of complete helplessness that had hit him out on the mound. He wondered why he had felt that way. He wondered if the attacks of nerves would ever end.

Coach Lasorda walked by him and ruffled his hair with his fingers. "Good game, Ramirez. I was kinda worried about you for a minute out there. You looked a little shaky. But you seemed to pull yourself together. That's the sign of a winner. I like that, kid. Keep up the good work."

"Thanks, Coach," Roberto smiled. "I'll try."

When the stocky manager left Magic flipped his shoes off and tugged hard on his socks to pull them off. "A little shaky . . . " he said, laughingly. "If only they knew. . . . "

TWO

David Green tugged his navy blue cap with the red-and-white *B* firmly down on his head. He took a deep breath, grabbed his glove, and walked from the Boston Red Sox' clubhouse, through the dimly lighted concrete corridor, and into the team's dugout. The bright sunshine hit his eyes, making him squint to see what he had dreamed of for years: Yankee Stadium.

Just called up to the Major Leagues from Pawtucket, David's opening action was going to be a three-game series against the famed New York Yankees. He stood dumbstruck at the foot of the dugout stairs, blankly soaking up the rich atmosphere of history and tradition.

It seemed like a long time ago that he was leading his Rosemont Rockets to a state championship. Now David was hoping to help the Boston Red Sox win a pennant.

"Hey, kid, what's the problem?"

David spun around and saw Roger Cowans looking at him with a smile on his face.

"Well . . . uh . . . I guess . . . nothing. Nothing's wrong!" David stammered nervously. "I was just looking around."

Cowans slapped him on the back and laughed. "I don't blame ya, Green." The ace of the Boston pitching staff looked around the stadium and sighed, "It still gets to me every time we come in here."

David felt relieved. "It seems a lot bigger than I even imagined. TV doesn't do it justice."

Cowans took a step up out of the dugout and David followed. "No way, man. TV can't capture the electricity of this place. I still remember my first trip out to the mound here like it was yesterday."

A long pause interrupted his words. David waited anxiously for him to continue.

"They get ya with their stadium. You can just feel the presence, of Ruth, Gehrig, Dimaggio, Mantle, Maris, Ford. Then they get ya when you see those pin stripes. I tell ya, it's tough to think of them as just another team when you play here. Just remember that and try not to get caught up in it," Cowans said.

David nodded as he continued to look around the field. "I'll try."

"Hey, Green. Front and center!"

David snapped to attention when he heard the voice of Joe Morgan, the Red Sox manager.

Morgan ran his fingers through his thinning gray hair before cocking his cap back on his head. He stuffed his hands into his navy blue warm-up jacket and turned toward his newest player. "Well, Green, whadya think? You ready to play?"

"Yes sir," David snapped back excitedly. "Can't wait!" Pictures of long home runs bouncing off the façade of the right-field upper deck came to David's mind.

"Then get on out to center field and check it out. We might need you for defensive purposes out there in the late innings, so be prepared."

Crestfallen, David loped out toward the outfield. "Defensive purposes in the late innings?" he sneered. "What about letting me do some offensive damage in the early innings?" he mumbled to himself.

When he reached the wall beyond center field, David peered over the fence and stared at the plaques commemorating the Yankees' greatest heroes. Lost in thought for a moment, he didn't hear the approach of one of his teammates.

"Hey, Rookie. Enough of that stuff!"

David twirled around and saw one of Boston's legends standing in front of him: Jim Ross. Lost for words, David pounded his glove and walked toward him.

"I'm supposed to help you out here," Ross said. "Manager's orders. Let's get to it."

David could tell by the edge in his voice that Ross wasn't happy to be out there. A former all-star center fielder for the Sox, he had lost a few steps at the hands of age. Now, it was a few games at first but mainly d-h-ing.

"I take it you've never been to Yankee Stadium before?" Ross asked.

"No, sir," gulped David.

Ross laughed. "You might as well cut the sir stuff now before someone else hears ya. I don't know who'd take more ribbing, you or me! Just call me Jim."

"Okay, Jim." David felt funny addressing someone he'd watched on television for years.

Ross pulled a ball out of his glove and walked toward the outfield wall. David fell in behind him.

"First thing to learn is the way the ball comes off the wall here. You've got some funny angles it'll bounce depending on where it hits."

Ross ripped a couple of hard throws into the padded wall to show how the ball would react. David scooped them up and tossed them back to his teacher.

"The thing you want to remember," Ross lectured, "is don't let the ball play you. You've gotta get into position and charge the ball. It's a long way back to the infield from back here in center so you've gotta hustle to make a play."

"Gotcha," David nodded.

His confidence both impressed and annoyed the Boston veteran.

"I heard you've got a pretty good arm. That's why they brought you up here, I think."

David felt a slow burn. "I used to be known for my hitting," he growled.

Ross laughed. "Hey, man, chill out. I'm sure you can hit. But it's defense the skipper's worried about. Down the stretch here we need to win every game we can, and offense isn't the only answer. Most of the time it's the team with the best pitching and defense that pulls it out."

Shrugging, David agreed. "Yeah, I know. I was just disappointed when Morgan told me I'd probably only go in during the late innings for defensive purposes. I think I can help with the bat, too. Now I wonder if I'll even get a chance to show it."

"Oh, you'll get a chance. Don't worry about that. And the best way to ensure that is to make yourself invaluable out here in the field. Then they'll have to play you all the time."

"You're right!" David said, nodding enthusiastically. "I never thought about that."

Ross threw a few more balls into the nooks and crannies of Yankee Stadium's center field fence. Satisfied that David was catching on, he called him back over again.

"Next thing to worry about tonight is the lights. They're pretty powerful, and if you look straight up into them you can blind yourself for a couple of seconds. If you don't wanna look stupid out here, figure out where the light poles are and get used to angling your vision away from the direct light. I'm sure you've seen what happens if you don't."

Laughing, David pictured in his mind a televised game he'd seen as a kid. The center fielder ended up taking a mad dash away from an easy pop fly, afraid he was going to be hit in the head, because he had lost it in the lights. "You're right about that. You can look pretty stupid out here."

Ross told him how to turn his body one way or the other, depending on the batter, so that he could avoid the problem. After that, they both headed back toward the dugout.

"Thanks, Jim. For everything," David said.

His sincerity won the veteran over. Ross slapped him hard across the shoulder. "You'll do okay, kid. Just remember, take what they give you and make the most of it. If it's just defensive cleanup in the late innings, make it count. You never know when the door will open for you."

"I'll remember that," David said.

David sat at the far corner of the Red Sox' dugout while he watched his team struggle against the Yankees. The score was tied 2-2 in the top of the eighth. When the regular Boston center fielder, Dwight Evert, flied out to end the inning, Joe Morgan made the big change.

"Green . . . go in at center!"

David jumped to his feet and grabbed his glove. Dashing out of the dugout, his heart started pumping as he glanced at the enormous crowd surrounding the field. He heard the PA announcer's words. "Now playing in center field for the Red Sox . . . David Green!"

Struggling to control his emotions, David jumped up and down in place to loosen up his muscles. When the left-hand-batting Don Satterly took his place in the batter's box, David angled his body toward right field and located the lights, as Ross had taught him. Muscles taut and throat dry, David anxiously awaited his first Major League action.

Satterly lined the first pitch he saw into right field for a single. David had raced over to back up the right fielder, but had no play to make. Returning to his position in center, he felt better after the long run.

When you get right down to it, this is just like baseball anywhere else, thought David. The plays are the same. The next three batters all grounded out meekly and left Mattingly stranded on the bases. As David loped back toward the dugout, the score remained tied.

Boston couldn't get anything going in its half of the inning, so when he took the field in the last half of the ninth David knew they had to hold the Yanks or the game would be over.

When the first two New Yorkers popped out on infield flies, David felt sure the game was going to extra innings. But his confidence changed suddenly when the next batter walked and immediately stole second. He knew now that any hit would probably score the run and win the game.

Dave Minnefield stepped back into the box after the stolen base. He pounded the plate with his bat and swung it menacingly several times to warm up. David was positive they were going to walk him. He was surprised when the first pitch was rifled in across the plate for a strike.

They must know something I don't, David thought.

Shading Minnefield slightly toward left, David moved a couple of feet in. He knew he'd need the extra steps to get to a single up the middle if he was to have any chance at getting the runner at home.

While all these thoughts raced through his mind, David was stunned when he heard the crack of the bat and the ball streaking out directly toward him.

Reacting even before he consciously knew what had happened, David tore in toward the infield. The sinking line drive was definitely over the infielders' heads, but David knew it wasn't going to reach him in time for a catch.

Out of the corner of his eye, he saw the runner rounding third. David lunged, made a short hop grab of the liner, and came up firing in a single motion.

His arm propelled the ball forward like a cannon shot. The throw honed in on home plate

like a cruise missile seeking its target. The
Boston catcher, Rick Waldman, braced himself
in front of the plate. The ball flew all the way to
home on the fly. It hit the catcher's glove at the
same instant that the Yankee runner hit the
catcher's leg. Waldman went down in a heap on
top of the runner as a cloud of dust rose up
around the play.

When the air settled, the umpire saw the
runner's leg inches short of the plate, and
Waldman's glove, with the ball still in it, resting on the Yankee's chest.

"You're outta here!" the ump screamed.

The Red Sox team let out a whoop and raced
into the dugout. David hit the dugout steps and
was mobbed by his new teammates.

"Wayda go, Rook!"

"Fantastic job, kid!"

"Bionic arm! Gotta be a bionic arm!"

David felt like a million bucks.

The commotion settled down, and Joe Morgan wandered toward his newest player. He
flipped David's cap off and ruffled up his hair.
"Nice work, Green."

"Thanks, Coach." was all David could say.

The Sox were retired without a run in the
tenth, but luckily the Yankees were too. The
score was still 2 apiece.

When the Red Sox got their first two runners on in the eleventh, David, knowing the
game was his to win, walked toward the
plate. The Yankees called time and their

manager went out to the mound. After he had consulted with the catcher, the signal went out to the bullpen for a reliever. David stepped back toward the on deck circle to continue warming up.

When the Yankee reliever took the mound Joe Morgan jumped out of the Red Sox dugout and walked toward the plate.

"Green," he called out.

Surprised, David turned around and looked at him. "Yeah?"

Morgan wagged his finger at him. "Take a seat, kid. I'm sending in a pinch hitter."

David was stunned. The look on his face was a cross between shock and anger.

Morgan patted him on the back. "Strictly percentages, kid. They're going with a lefty so I'm countering with a right handed batter. You did your job, Green."

Depressed, David wandered back to the bench in a fog. He plopped down at the end of the dugout, his heroics of two innings ago completely forgotten.

Jim Ross came and sat down next to him.

When David didn't move Ross bumped into his shoulder. "Hey, Green. Don't sweat it. It wasn't anything against you."

"I can hit lefties. What's the big deal?"

Ross smiled. "We all can, Green . . . from down here. It's the manager's job to make that call. It's your job to do what he says."

"Yeah . . . some job," David grumbled. "A hero one minute . . . forgotten the next."

Ross laughed. "Welcome to the majors!"

THREE

Glen Mitchell, nicknamed Scrapper, stretched out on the trainer's table in the Chicago White Sox' clubhouse, waiting for his daily tape job. The hustling, all-out style of play he'd learned at Rosemont High had brought Glen several bumps, bruises, and nagging injuries. But he was winning over his teammates with his passion as the White Sox won more and more ball games.

"You tired of seeing me around here yet?" he asked the trainer as he began his routine. At sixty-two and with over forty years in baseball, Joey Digregorio had seen and heard it all.

Joey's round face lit up in a smile. "Naw. You're kinda fun to have everyday. You rookies will put up will all my old jokes. You even laugh at 'em. The vets around here just groan and moan while I'm working on 'em."

His short, fat, gnarled fingers quickly whipped the roll of tape around Glen's sore ankle. The trainer's skill made every move seem effortless.

"The way those guys complain," Joey continued, "you'd think they were dying. But I don't see any of them putting out half as much effort as you do when you're playing."

"Oh, they probably just like to give you a bad time. They're hustling out there just like me," said Glen.

"Maybe now they are. You've shamed them into it. You made some of these guys look bad, and they're scrambling to save their jobs. This is the first time we've been in a pennant race for some time. A lot of these jokers are just starting to realize what it takes to make it through the pressure cooker we're gonna be in."

"You've seen a few in your day, haven't ya, Joey?"

"You'd better believe it," he said as he cut the tape and neatly squared off the finish. "And trust me when I tell you it's been your influence these last few weeks that makes me think we've got a chance again."

Glen almost blushed. "Thanks, Joey. You're my biggest fan, I'll bet."

"You're gonna have a lot more before this season's over if we can keep up the pace. You just keep hustling your buns off and I'll keep you taped together so you can play. You and me, kid, we'll pull this team through."

Glen raised his hand for a high-five. Joey slapped it hard and Glen returned the hit. "You got it, man," Glen said. After we take out the Tigers tonight, we can make up some ground on Oakland when they come in tomorrow."

Joey scolded him. "Don't ever think about tomorrow, Scrapper. In this game it only matters what happens today."

"Hey, there's nothing wrong with making a few plans, is there?"

Shaking his head, Joey pushed Glen off the table. "As long as you remember where you are . . . and not be consumed with where you're going. You listen to me, kid!"

Glen nodded silently. But his thoughts brought a smile to his face. He didn't say the words but his mind was fixed on one thing — an American League Championship Series against his old teammate and one of his best friends, David Green, and the Boston Red Sox.

I'm waiting, DT, he thought. *I want you!*

The September evening in Chicago brought clear skies and a comfortably warm temperature — a perfect night for a ball game. The lights were already on in Comiskey Park even though a fair amount of daylight remained. The stands were filling up with fans who eagerly anticipated this important game in the Sox' pennant drive.

Scrapper paced around the bag at second base. He was anxious for the game to start. When the pitcher finally finished taking his warm-ups, Glen sighed with relief as the catcher's throw came to him. "Okay, guys. Let's go. Let's go!" he hollered.

The Tigers' first three batters all went down meekly. The crowd cheered wildly, as if the Sox had already won the game.

Scrapper and Chicago's shortstop Rick Finnigan ran in toward the dugout.

"Geez . . . you think the crowd's fired up or what?" Scrapper asked his teammate.

Rick looked up toward the stands. It was his fourth year with the Sox, but he had never seen anything like this. "Nuts! They're going nuts. I wonder what this place is gonna be like if we win the pennant."

"When!" Scrapper corrected him. "It's when we win the pennant. Don't forget that."

The tension was evident in the Sox' players as well as Detroit's. Chicago's batters were retired easily as well. Scrapper's fly ball to left field was the only ball well hit in the first inning.

The game quickly settled into a defensive struggle with both pitchers dominating the game. When Glen walked in the sixth, stole second, and scored on a single by first baseman Rudy York, it looked like that one run might be enough to win the game. When Chicago took the field in the top of the ninth, all they had to do was shut down the Tigers to win 1-0. When Chicago's starting pitcher, "Lefty" Cummens, walked the first man he faced, the Sox bullpen scrambled to attention. When the second batter ripped a hard shot down the third base line for a single, the call went out for a reliever.

Glen cussed under his breath and scraped at the dirt in front of him. "What's going on? We only need three rotten outs. Three rotten outs!"

Scrapper edged his way over toward Finnigan. "Hey, Finny!" He waved his shortstop closer to him. "Left handed batter coming up, so you cover second if they try something. They probably won't, but keep alert."

Rick resented the younger player's lecture. "Listen, kid. I know how the game's played. You stay alert and take care of your business. I'll take care of mine!"

Scrapper seemed surprised by the hostile tone of his voice. He edged back toward his position and waited for the reliever to finish his warm-ups. "Tension must be getting to everybody," he muttered to himself.

The Tigers' Jake Myers stepped into the box.

The crowd noise rose several decibels as the pitcher started his windup. The pitch started out over the plate and sailed in on the batter. His weak swing produced a pop foul that the catcher easily handled. One out. "Thatta way. Thatta way," the infielders cheered. Glen held up one finger and turned toward the outfielders. "One gone. One gone!"

And two to go, Glen thought. *We can win this division race yet. Then it's only one more step to the World Series!* Glen wanted it so badly he could taste it. His father had never played in a World Series Championship. This would be one way finally to distance himself from his father's accomplishments.

But the next Tigers batter didn't want to cooperate. Refusing to swing at bad pitches, he worked the count carefully and earned a base on balls. This loaded up the bases, and there was still only one out. An audible groan arose from the stands.

"Double play now," Glen screamed. "Any base . . . force at any base."

The players looked around at each other. The strain on their face was obvious.

Having won the world championship a few years earlier, the Tigers were no strangers to winning important ball games. Now, with the game on the line, an eager, ready to play attitude showed in their eyes. Frank Thomas stepped to the plate and slammed his bat down hard on the plate. The Sox reliever worked from the stretch, since that was what he was used to. He checked the runners to make sure they didn't get too big a lead. He stared down at his catcher and fired.

Thomas caught the pitch right on the screws. He sent a sharp line drive back through the box, and the relief pitcher had to scramble to avoid being hurt.

The ball looked like a sure base hit. But Glen had other ideas. His mind calculated the angle to pursue and cut off the hard smash. He dove at the edge of the infield grass, and his outstretched glove just hung on to the ball.

Scrambling to his feet, he hurled a perfect strike to Finnigan who was covering second, to easily get the runner coming down. Finnegan glided across the bag and fired the relay toward first.

Glen couldn't believe his eyes. He watched as the wildly thrown ball sailed into the Chicago dugout and the umpire waved the runners forward. First, one run scored to tie the game. Then the second Tiger hit home plate and they took the lead, 2-1.

Glen jumped to his feet and brushed the dirt and grass off his uniform. As he walked by Finnigan, he lifted his shoulders and hands and stared at him with puzzled eyes. "What're ya doing! What kinda throw was that?" Finnigan ignored him and walked with his head down back to short. When the next batter was retired, the Sox, obviously a beaten team, trotted back toward their dugout.

Chicago's manager, Joe Walsh, tried to pump his players back up. "C'mon guys. We've still got our at bats here. Let's fire up and get those runs back!"

But his words fell on deaf ears. One look around the dugout told Glen that his teammates had already packed it in for the day.

Three up and three down later, the results were final. Detroit 2 . . . Chicago 1.

Glen was furious. He'd never played with a group that didn't die trying. It wasn't his style and it wasn't going to be.

As the team walked into the clubhouse, Glen couldn't contain himself. He turned toward Finnigan and put his finger on the shortstop's chest.

"You'd better get your head screwed on straight, buddy. There's no damn excuse for a throw like that. You cost us this game!"

Finnigan ignored Glen's comments and headed for his locker.

Glen wouldn't let it go. "I told you to be ready! What were ya thinking out there?"

Several of the other Sox spoke up. "Zip it, Mitchell. Rick feels bad enough without you harping on him."

"Save your speeches, kid. You're just a rookie around here and don't forget it."

The blood rose in Glen's neck. He couldn't believe anyone would defend the careless play. "I'm not the one who just threw this game down the toilet, brickheads! How in the world are we gonna get anywhere with stupid plays like that?"

Finnigan rose from his bench in front of his locker and threw a towel at Glen. "Lay off, Mitchell. Don't tell us you've never made any mistakes."

Glen exploded. He leaped forward and grabbed Finnigan by the neck, knocking him to the ground. The two players rolled around on the carpeted floor while their teammates encircled them.

Cheers and jeers filled the air as the two infielders struggled to get the upper hand.

The Sox manager heard the commotion and dashed into the clubhouse from his office. Pushing his way past the onlookers, he fought his way to the center of the battle.

"What the hell's going on here?" he screamed. With one giant hand he plucked Rick up from the ground and pinned him against a locker. Turning his attention to Glen, Walsh scooped his second baseman up and put a hammerlock on his head. "So, ya wanta fight, Mitchell," the manager grunted as he struggled to contain Glen. "Then how about fighting me?"

Glen's temper almost drove him to it. But an attack of common sense finally started to overcome his emotions. He slowly went limp in the grasp of his manager.

"Smart choice, kid," Walsh said as he pushed Glen to the opposite side of the aisle. "Now, who's gonna tell me what's going on . . . as if I didn't know?"

Everybody fell silent.

Walsh hesitated only for a second. "Then I'll tell all of you. You guys blew one today. We had a chance to push the Tigers another step away from their division lead and boost ourselves another game closer in our division. Instead we let it get away."

Turning toward Glen, Walsh continued. "And, Mr. Hotshot — Joe Mitchell's son here — took it upon himself to punish whoever he blamed for the loss. Am I right?"

Not waiting for an answer, Walsh stared down each one of his players and then concentrated on Glen. "Well I wanna know why you settled on Finnigan. Did you forget who signaled for that pitch that got hit? And what about the guy who threw it? Or maybe me, since I chose the reliever? Think about all those possibilities, Mitchell. Because I'm thinking about why the hell you didn't get a few more hits and maybe help put this game outta reach before the ninth inning since you're so dang perfect. Whadya say about that?"

Glen hung his head and stood silently.

Walsh started walking away but stopped. He turned back toward all of his players. "This is a team game, gentlemen. And we're gonna win as a team or lose as a team. That choice is pretty much up to you. We've come this far . . . it'd be a shame to back away from it now."

He waited for his words to sink in. "As for you Mitchell. I know you want to win. I haven't got a complaint about that. But you'd better figure out a way to communicate that desire without ripping your teammates apart. You can sit on the bench during tomorrow's game and think about it!"

Glen sank to the ground, his back scraping against the locker as he slid down.

His teammates didn't say anything as they slowly dispersed and headed for the showers.

Glen's head sank into his hands. He'd never felt any lower. "I've blown it! My big chance in the majors and I've really blown it!"

All the dreams of a play-off against David and a possible World Series ring came crashing down on him. As the regular noise level of the locker room picked up again, Glen fought back the tears he felt forming. Taking a deep breath, he pulled himself together. He wasn't going to let anyone see him like that, he decided. And he wasn't going to let his season end this way.

FOUR

The Los Angeles Dodgers were annoyed, not angry. They weren't worried, just a little upset. Their drive toward the Western Division championship had been slowed, not derailed. There wasn't any reason for concern.

Roberto Ramirez sat in the locker room before that night's game with the Cincinnati Reds, reading the *Los Angeles Times* sports section. The box scores told the story. Four straight losses by the Dodgers, and four straight wins by the Astros. Los Angeles still hadn't clinched the division. Now, with only eight games left, some people were actually talking about mathematical possibilities.

A group of Dodgers ballplayers were deeply engrossed in their daily card game. Others worked on their equipment. Several of the players had to spend time in physical therapy, fighting off the effects of the 162-game schedule.

Nobody seemed overly worried, except manager Tommy Lasorda. He paced up and down the carpeted floor of the clubhouse and pored over a mountain of statistics in his hands.

"Hey, Coach," one of the players yelled out from the safety of a crowd. "Give it a rest. You're wearing a hole there where you're pacing!" Lasorda stopped . . . right next to Roberto. He leaned over and swore, "I'm gonna get that guy!"

Roberto looked up in amazement. His mind was on the game that he was about to start, and he was fighting off a case of pregame jitters. But he didn't think the comment was so bad. He was surprised his coach seemed so angry.

"Gee, Coach. He didn't mean anything by it, I'm sure."

Lasorda looked at Roberto crossly. Then he realized his rookie didn't understand.

"No, no, no, no, Ramirez. You've got it all wrong. I guess you weren't with us on our last eastern road trip."

"No . . . sorry. I missed it." Roberto was puzzled.

"That's the joker who got me, and I swore, when the time was right . . . there'd be a payback!"

"What'd he do?"

Lasorda lowered his voice, as if sharing a deep secret. "We were staying in the Essex House in New York. We'd just beaten the Mets in the first game of the series, and everyone was loose and happy. I'm positive it was Marshfield's idea. Anyway, all the players went around gathering up the room service dishes. This was around one in the morning, mind ya."

Roberto started to smile. He could feel that Lasorda had a great deal of respect for whatever happened.

"Anyway," Lasorda continued, "they carefully pile up all the dishes against my door. I mean they've got a cart carefully tipped up against it, and a ton of glasses and plates and silverware, all neatly balanced and arranged."

Roberto could see it coming.

"So I get the phone call from Henderson . . . wakes me up in the middle of the night . . . to tell me he's got a problem that he needs to talk to me about. Noooooo . . . it can't wait until morning. So I pull on a pair of pants and head for the door. When I open it . . . Geez, the noise must have woke up everybody in the hotel . . . and I think I've been shot. I mean I don't know what's happening. Here I am covered with dirty dishes, ice cubes, and garbage."

Roberto fell off the bench laughing.

"Well, I promised that I'd get even and I'm just waiting for the right time. Rest assured . . . I'll get 'em."

The story had Roberto in stitches. All worries about the game against Cincinnati had disappeared. As Lasorda wandered off to plan his strategy, the rookie Dodger right-hander calmly started to get dressed for the ball game.

The fashionable L.A. crowd began filing into Dodger Stadium earlier than usual. Restless with their team's four-game losing streak, they were anxious to clinch the division and had turned out in force for this last home game of the season. After this game, the Dodgers faced a season-ending road trip to Atlanta and Houston.

Roberto took his warm-ups out in the bullpen while his team practiced fielding. He felt rusty. Since joining the Dodgers he was pitching only every fifth game, and his arm wasn't used to the inactivity. He preferred to go every fourth day.

As he tried to iron the kinks out of his throwing motion, the Dodgers's pitching coach approached him.

"Well, kid. This is a big game tonight."

Roberto didn't want to listen. He had not hit it off with Dave Westrum since joining the big league team. There was just something in Westrum's manner that got under Roberto's skin.

"I'm ready, Coach," Magic responded.

"You'd better be. I think the crowd's restless for a win. They'll probably get all over you if you screw up." The edge in Westrum's voice made his comments seem like little digs.

Roberto shrugged and avoided eye contact with his coach. "If we get a few runs, nobody will even notice me. We'll just cruise like we were earlier, before this little slump."

"Hope you're right, Rookie," Westrum chortled. "But don't count on an easy game from the Reds. They fight and claw and dig for everything they get. They've got the personality of their manager . . . old Pete Rose! They're gonna make your life miserable if they can."

The muscles around Roberto's stomach started to tighten. All of Lasorda's pregame efforts to relax his pitcher were starting to disappear. Magic wondered if Westrum just didn't like him.

Roberto swatted the ball out of the air as his catcher threw it back to him. He turned and headed for the dugout. He'd heard enough. He wanted to get away from the source of his irritation. When he reached the infield, Lasorda hopped out of the dugout.

"You warmed up, Ramirez?" the manager asked.

"Well enough. If I'd stayed out there any longer I would have gotten too hot."

The tone in his voice left little to the imagination about his mood.

"Hey, kid. C'mon over here." Lasorda waved his hand and wagged his finger.

Roberto reluctantly went to his side.

"Stay loose out there. I don't know what happened but don't let anyone get to you. Stay in control."

Magic nodded.

Lasorda recalled his pitcher's last outing and the obvious mental struggle he went through. "Just don't forget there's eight other guys out there to help. Don't take on the weight of the world. This is a team game, remember."

"Yeah . . . okay." Roberto started breathing more slowly again.

"I've got all the faith in the world in ya, Rook. I know you can do it. Just relax and let it happen."

Roberto stepped down into the dugout and found a seat on the bench. He let his mind wander back over the past couple of years and some of the big games he'd thrown before.

"I'll show 'em," he said to himself.

When the public-address announcer finally introduced the lineups Roberto was ready. When the Dodgers took the field he sprinted out to the mound. He looked around the field and the swollen stands and smiled.

This is great! he thought. He threw down the rosin bag and took his nine warm-up tosses. When the first batter stepped into the box, Roberto had completely forgotten about Coach Westrum. All he concentrated on was the seventeen-inch-wide slab of white rubber laying sixty feet, six inches away from him.

Taking his windup, he uncorked his first pitch. The ball streaked across the inside corner of the plate. The crowd could hear the ball pop into the catcher's glove and then the umpire's loud call.

" *Striiiiiiiiike* one!"

After a quick glance in for the sign, Roberto rifled another bullet in across the plate. Again the call was a strike.

The crowd had already started cheering.

Roberto could feel the adrenaline pulsing through his body. He and his catcher were on the same wavelength on the next signal. The curve ball came screaming in toward home as had his first two fastballs. But just as the batter was about to make contact, the ball's trajectory broke down, as if the ball had been pulled away on a string.

"Striiiiiike three . . . you're outta here!" the umpire hollered.

The crowd went nuts.

Lasorda turned to his pitching coach sitting next to him on the bench. "The kid looks like he's got good stuff today."

Westrum cocked his head. "Yeah . . . let's just hope he can keep it up."

Two more quick strikeouts and the Reds were retired. Magic left the mound to the cheers of the fans and the support of his teammates.

"Wayda go, Ramirez."

"Atta baby . . . atta baby," Lasorda yelled out from the dugout.

The Dodger catcher Steve Henderson lumbered in toward the dugout and met Roberto at the top step. "Good stuff, kid. Those balls are really popping in there!"

Magic smiled. "Thanks. I feel strong today."

Henderson shook his glove hand and blew on it. "That's an understatement, man. You're feeling really strong!"

Pumped up by their pitcher's strong start, the Dodgers immediately went to work on Cincinnati's ace, Dave Humm. A single, stolen base, double, another single, and a home run produced a quick 4-0 lead. When Roberto took the mound in the second inning, he'd never felt more confident.

As the game progressed, Magic's arm got better and better. Spotting his pitches at will, he retired the first eighteen batters in order. Through six innings, the score grew to 7-0.

The Dodgers' bench was caught in an unusual situation. Ready to explode and celebrate their almost clinched division championship, they were held silent by the suspense and tension created by the perfect game. The time honored baseball tradition of not talking about it kept everyone on the edge of his seat.

Walking to the pitcher's rubber in the top of the seventh, Roberto glanced up at the scoreboard and saw the long string of zeros. The line read:

Reds 000 000 = 0 0 0

L.A. 401 020 = 7 9 0

After striking out the lead-off batter, Roberto punched the air with his fist. He was caught up in the possibility of a perfect game. The crowd roared after every pitch.

The next two Reds hitters both grounded out to second base and the fans erupted in cheers. There were only six more outs to go.

Roberto sat next to his battery mate, Henderson, and tried to talk to him about the game.

"Two more innings, Steve. Do ya think we can do it?" he asked.

Henderson looked at him in amazement. "Geez, Rookie. Don't you know any better than to be talking 'bout it? It's bad luck."

Roberto laughed. "Luck is all there is to it, whether we talk about it or not. Hey, relax! I'm the one who's supposed to be nervous."

Henderson punched him in the shoulder . . . of his glove-hand arm. "The way you're throwing, luck's got almost nothing to do with it."

"Oh, c'mon. Any one of those balls that have been hit could have been right in between the fielders rather than at 'em. My next pitch might be perfect and the batter might bloop it off the end of his bat for a single. Who's to say? You can't worry about that kinda stuff."

"Geez, you're amazing. You throw a lot of perfect games in your life that maybe I don't know about?"

Magic laughed again. "Let's just win. I wanna get to the play-offs . . . that's what's important." He let his mind wander for a split second. A shot at either David Green or Glen Mitchell, his two best friends, helped to motivate him.

The three quick outs in the top of the eighth did nothing to alleviate the pressure and tension. Dodger Stadium was like a time bomb ready to explode. Nobody on the L.A. bench would even look at his teammates as they batted in the bottom of the eighth.

Only one man remained unfazed by what was happening: Roberto Ramirez. He amazed and confounded everyone by continuing to talk to and needle his teammates about trivial things. When he left the dugout to start the last inning Lasorda turned to Westrum and shrugged. "Must just be his way to deal with the pressure," the manager reasoned.

"He's an odd one," Westrum said. "He's either one cool cucumber or he's a heckuva actor."

Lasorda nodded. "He sure doesn't seem like the same kid who pitched last week. One game he's as nervous as a mouse at a cat show and the next he looks like the cat. One thing's for sure. No matter what's going on in his mind, the kid can flat out throw the baseball!"

The Dodgers fans gave Roberto a standing ovation as he took the field for the last inning. After his warm-ups, Magic paused a moment to let his eyes circle the stadium and soak in the drama of what was happening.

Taking his windup, Roberto fired the first pitch in to the batter and listened as it popped into the catcher's glove.

"Striiiiike one!" the umpire bellowed.

The fans went crazy. Those who were listening to their radios heard the broadcasters say, "That last pitch by Ramirez was clocked at ninety-eight miles per hour. Whew!"

Magic nodded when he saw the next sign. *Perfect,* he thought.

His arm came whipping toward the plate with his delivery. When the ball left his hand, it seemed another fastball was on its way. But the pitch was a change-up. Meant to fool the batter, it did just that. Cincinnati's Caesar Mendoza swung before the ball was halfway to the plate. But as luck would have it, he checked his swing just enough to catch a piece of it off the end of his bat. A slow knuckling dribbler came rolling off his bat down the first base line.

Instantly, Roberto, Henderson, and the first baseman took off toward the ball. The second baseman headed for first to cover the bag. All three Dodgers reached the ball at the same time and realized immediately there was no play at first on the fleet-footed Mendoza. Their only chance was to let the ball go foul.

As the swinging bunt rolled down the line, it curved toward the foul line, tantalizingly brushing it for an instant and then trickling back into play. It rolled dead five feet from first, not more than three inches fair. The perfect game was over.

The crowd let out a collective groan, but then slowly rose to its feet and started another standing ovation. When the next batter bounced into a game ending double play, the fans poured out onto the field to celebrate the Western Conference title with their players.

Mobbed by both his fans and teammates, Roberto struggled to get off the field and into the clubhouse. His hat missing and his white jersey ripped, he finally dove into the protected area.

"Fantastic, Ramirez! Heckuva ball game, kid. Too bad about the perfect game, though!" said Lasorda. Roberto smiled. "We won, Coach. Who could ask for anything more? We've got a chance at the World Series now!" And to himself, he added, " . . .a shot at a Rosemont reunion to boot!"

FIVE

David Green tried his best to be patient. The Boston Red Sox were winning, but he was sitting on the bench. It was a situation that met with only half of his approval. It was also a situation that he had never faced before.

Since his first year in Little League ball, all the way through high school at Rosemont High, David had been a star. Stuck on the bench as a platoon player, only facing right-handed pitchers, didn't make David very happy. He knew he could handle his position full time.

He had done fairly well when given the chance against righties. It was bewildering to him that they thought he wouldn't do the same against left-handers. But entering the final game of the season, he'd all but given up hope of making it as a full time player for the Sox.

The tension of the pennant race had everyone on edge. Boston found themselves in a heat-
ed battle with the Yankees and the Tigers for
the Eastern Division crown. Throughout the
last three weeks of the season, the teams had
traded places at the top.

Boston went into the last day of the season
needing a win to clinch the pennant. Playing at
home in front of a huge crowd, on a beautiful,
clear New England day, made everything seem
perfect.

The mood in the clubhouse before the game
had combined tension, anxiety, and hope. Confidence seemed to be the one thing missing.

"Okay, guys, gather round for a second,"
manager Joe Morgan said.

From the various corners of the spacious,
well-appointed locker room, the players assem-
bled in front of their leader.

"I don't have to tell you guys what this
means today. We have our destiny in our own
hands and you can't have it any better than
that. It doesn't matter what anyone else does
today; all we have to do is win."

A few scattered cries of, "Right On" arose
from the players.

Morgan continued, "You guys have given me
everything I could hope for this season. Hustle,
hard work, heads up play and good attitudes
have gotten us through . . . "

David quickly thought about his own attitude.

" . . .and I know that whatever happens today, we can say that we've given it everything we've got. After the game, whether we win or lose, there probably won't be a chance for me to say this, so I wanted to say it now. Thanks!"

The players clapped loudly.

"We've still got one more win in us, Coach," a voice cried out. Morgan's head perked up. His voice rose as he spoke. "All right, then! Let's go out and do it!"

The Red Sox, brimming with confidence, jumped up and ran out of the clubhouse to take the field. Morgan's soft spoken pep talk had been just the medicine they needed.

Their opponents, the Toronto Blue Jays, had suffered through a disappointing season. Picked in the preseason to be a force in the American League East, they had struggled all year to play .500 ball. The last two weeks of the season, though, they had been playing the roll of spoilers.

First they'd knocked off the Yankees in a three game series. Then they pummeled Detroit, three out of four. Now they were looking to close out the season on a positive note and make life miserable for the Red Sox.

When the Sox took the field, the Boston fans stood and gave them a tremendous reception. The organist fired up his musical intro and the announcer blared out, "Ladies and gentlemen, your Boston Red Sox!"

Sitting on the bench, David felt goose bumps run up and down his spine. As his eyes roamed around the storied old stadium, he fought back tears.

"I wish I could be out there," he sighed to himself.

The coaches paced nervously up and down the dugout floor, their hands stuffed in their navy blue warm-up jackets. All of the substitute players were screaming out their encouragement. All except David. All he could do was sit and stare.

When Toronto's lead-off batter stepped into the box, the decibel level of the crowd rose. After the first pitch, a strike, it sounded as if Boston had won the game.

"Geez, this is amazing," David said to no one in particular.

"This is pennant fever, kid," said one of the veterans, leaning against the rail a few feet from the rookie center fielder. "Ain't nothing like it!"

The crowd was quickly silenced, though, on the next pitch. Billy Ray North lashed a single up the middle to start things off for the Blue Jays.

When the next batter popped out behind the plate the fans got right back into their festive mood, which grew even brighter when the Blue Jays' power hitting right fielder struck out.

But with two out and a runner on first, George Sales ripped a towering blast over the

Green Monster in left field, and Toronto
jumped up 2-0. The crowd managed only polite
applause when the final out was recorded to
end the top of the first.

"Okay, guys. No big deal. We can get 'em
right back," Morgan hollered to his troops as
they returned from the field. "Let's get on
'em!"

The players maintained their high spirits.
But when they were retired one, two, three in
their half of the first, it took something out of
them. Confidence was slowly giving way to
fear.

As an observer, rather than a participant,
David watched the subtle change in his teammates as the innings progressed. When Toronto
scored another run in the fourth to make it 3-0,
morale in the Sox' dugout really started to
sink.

Realizing that he wanted to contribute in
some way, David's natural leadership returned. As the Sox came to bat in the bottom of
the sixth, he jumped up from his seat on the
bench and walked up and down the dugout,
slapping his teammates on the back and trying
to fire them up.

"C'mon guys. Three runs is nothing. We can
explode right by these bums."

A few players seemed to join in his enthusi-
asm.

"Yeah. He's right! We're not dead. We've just gotta get up and start kicking some Blue Jay feathers."

Joe Morgan watched David's attempt to motivate his teammates. He was impressed by the rookie's spirit.

"Green's right, you guys. We've just got to relax and go out and do what we're capable of doing . . . scoring runs."

The players started clapping and hollering as the first Sox batter stepped into the box. Their excitement leaped when Mike Kelly rapped a double into the right-field corner.

"Thatta way! Thatta way!"

"Here we go, now! Keep it up!" When Bobby Johnson lifted a high fly ball toward the right field wall, the players and fans rose to their feet. At the warning track, right up against the fence, the Blue Jays right fielder leaped high and speared the ball for an out. But Kelly scampered down to third after tagging up, so Boston had a runner in scoring position with only one out.

"Let's bring him home now," Morgan yelled.

David screamed out to Mike Ross as he walked toward the plate. "Take it downtown, Ross. You can do it!"

David had a funny feeling when he heard himself use his own nickname, Downtown. 'I'd sure as heck show 'em what downtown means," he said softly.

Ross, a picture of power and concentration up at the plate, took the first pitch and nailed it. His short, compact, but devastating swing made solid contact, and the ball soared out toward center field.

Pulled just a little more, or sliced slightly right, the ball would have made an easy home run. But the Blue Jays center fielder raced all the way back to the center field wall and made the catch for the second out.

Kelly easily loped in from third for the first Sox run. The crowd was disappointed that it wasn't a home run, but it was thrilled to get its first run. The inning ended with the next batter grounding out, but now a 3-1 score was up on the board. "Nice try," David yelled as center fielder Ross grabbed his glove and headed out toward the field.

"Thanks, Rook. I heard ya yelling for me in here while I was walking to the plate."

"Never hurts to give a little support," David said, smiling.

"You're okay, kid. You're gonna do just fine."

Ross ran out toward center and David returned to his seat on the bench.

Boston's manager came and sat beside him.

"That's the way to stay in the game, Green. I like your attitude," he said.

"Thanks, Coach. I'm ready if you need me."

Morgan flipped David's cap back on his head. "I know it, Rookie. You don't have to tell me."

The Blue Jays started off the seventh with another single. When the count went to 3 and 0 on the next batter, Morgan stood up and started pacing up and down the dugout. He knew that any more scoring by the Jays would stop the momentum his team was starting to build.

He grabbed the phone to the bullpen on the wall at the end of the dugout. "Better get Leonetti and Washington warmed up," he growled into the receiver.

The Boston starter saw the bullpen activity and knew he'd better not walk anyone. He grooved his next pitch right down the middle of the plate. David watched the Toronto batter jump on the pitch and send a long fly ball out toward left center. Both Ross and O'Meara, the left fielder, took off on a dead run for the ball.

From David's point of view, it looked like a sure double off the wall. But Ross, despite his age, made a mad dash to make the play. Just as the ball was about to carom off the Green Monster, Ross jumped and got his glove on it.

The ball, Ross, and the wall all met in a terrible crash. Boston's center fielder went down in a heap and O'Meara raced over to help. When he got to the scene of the collision, Ross was writhing on the ground, but the ball was still in his glove. Fishing it out of Ross's webbing, O'Meara turned and fired the ball back into the infield, and they doubled off the runner for the second out.

By the time order was restored, the whole Boston team was standing out in center field, anxiously looking over their fallen star.

The Boston trainer examined Ross and knew immediately what the problem was. He turned to Morgan and said, "Separated shoulder . . . he's not gonna be available till next spring!"

Morgan nodded, then quickly turned toward his newest player. "Green?"

"Yes, sir," David said as he snapped to attention.

"Grab your glove. It's your position now." David rolled his hand into a fist and punched the air. "All right."

"Hey, Rookie!" David heard a voice call out as he was heading to the dugout for his glove.

He turned around and saw Ross struggling to stand up, motioning toward him.

David walked toward him and said, "Unbelievable catch, Mike!"

Ross tried to smile. "Good luck out there, kid. I know you can do it."

"Thanks."

"Hey . . . it never hurts to give a little support, does it?" Ross said through clenched teeth.

When play resumed, the Blue Jays were now the team with the wind taken out of their sails. The spectacular catch by Ross and the subsequent double play killed their rally. The next batter up meekly grounded out to end the inning.

Boston came up with fire and determination, but they ran right up against Toronto's right-handed starter, who was still very strong. He struck out two batters and got the third to foul out. After seven innings the score was still 3-1 for the Jays.

It stayed that way until the bottom of the eighth. The Sox were sending up the meat of their order with their second, third, and clean up hitters.

David Green, who replaced Ross, was that clean up hitter, now due up. When the first batter of the eighth walked, the team felt like this was it . . . their best chance. Bobby Johnson followed the walk to Kelly with a clean single up the middle. As David walked toward the batter's box, the Toronto manager called time.

David's shoulders slumped when he saw the signal for a relief pitcher. He knew they'd bring in their ace left-hander, Al Sobronski, and he knew that meant a trip to the bench for him.

Morgan yelled out from the dugout to David as the reliever came in to warm up. "Green!"

David walked back to his manager.

"Okay, listen up, Green. Sobronski doesn't know anything about you so he'll stick with his bread and butter . . . the screwball."

David's eyes lit up. "You're leaving me in?" he asked in disbelief.

"Don't you think you can do it?" Morgan shot back at him.

"You betcha I can do it," David shouted. "All right!"

"Now listen to me. Try to lay off that screwball and make him throw strikes to ya."

David remembered his lessons back in A ball. "No problem, Coach."

"And Green," Morgan called out as his young hitter walked toward the plate. "Don't try and do it all yourself. Okay?"

David cocked his bat in the air and waved. When he took his stance in the batter's box, the PA blared out, "Now batting for the Sox . . . David Green."

A smattering of applause and cheers greeted him. Although they didn't know much about him, the fans were unwavering in their hopes that he would somehow deliver.

"Okay, David," he said to himself, taking a deep breath. "Stand up straight . . . relax . . . wait for your pitch!"

Sobronski started him off as expected. The screwball came in looking good, but David laid off of it. It broke down and inside for a ball.

"Good eye . . . good eye!" his teammates cried out.

The next pitch was a carbon copy of the first. Again, it looked good coming in, but David knew it would break low and inside, so he stood with the bat on his shoulder.

"Ball two," signaled the umpire.

David watched Sobronski kick the rubber. *Okay, David ol' boy, you've got him now!* he thought.

The Boston crowd was going nuts. They knew that the whole season was riding on the next few pitches.

"C'mon, Green," they screamed. "Get on base . . . wayda look up there!"

When Sobronski went into his stretch and checked the runners at first and second, David knew instinctively what the pitch was going to be. *It's gonna be the curve,* he reasoned. *He'll be afraid to test me with a fastball and knows he can throw the curve over the plate!* When the pitch left the Jays reliever's hand, David locked on the rotation of the ball and nodded to himself.

He no longer heard the crowd's screams. The splash of colors surrounding the field faded into black. All David could see or hear was the ball, lazily floating toward him.

He started his swing in what seemed like slow motion. His wrists cocked and forearms stiffened. His hips rolled through and brought the full force of his power into the impact zone, just in front of the plate.

The bat met the ball absolutely, squarely. The slight uppercut trajectory of this swing lifted the ball into upward flight. When he dropped the bat and started to run toward first, David slowly became aware of the crowd noise once again.

The fans were going berserk. Even before he could see it with his eyes, the crowd told David the ball was gone. As he rounded first base, the air in Fenway Park became filled with confetti, paper, seat cushions, hats, and anything else that could be thrown.

He didn't know until he was told later, but as he approached second base David started skipping and leaping into the air. The runners in front of him touched home and turned to wait for their teammate.

When he finally reached the plate David's fellow players swarmed around him. Hands reached over the pile to swat him on the back or head. The tears that formed in his eyes were from sheer, unbelieving joy.

"All right! All right!" his teammates screamed. "Fantastic! Outta sight!"

The superlatives didn't seem strong enough.

The Boston Red Sox batboy tried to work his way through the crowd to congratulate David. When he reached his side, he looked up and smiled. "Master Blaster!"

David laughed.

The top of the ninth was a foregone conclusion. Toronto went up and down, one, two, three. Boston won the Eastern Division championship.

As the celebration went on well into the night, David got swept away in the excitement. The party switched from the field to the club-

better. Then it hit him. Glen Mitchell's Chicago
White Sox. Could it be possible? An ALCS
against old teammates? "Geez, I almost forgot." He scrambled over to the bar and asked
no one in particular, "Hey . . . who won the
American League West?"

SIX

After his fight with Finnigan Glen Mitchell's Chicago White Sox played like a team on fire. Averaging only 4.35 runs per game before the dugout explosion, the Sox were now scoring at a 6.75 clip. The pitching staff had tightened up their ERAs, and everything was going their way.

After his one game suspension and an apology to his team, Glen got his spot back in the starting lineup. In the final games of the season, he had been on as much of a tear as his teammates.

On the final Sunday of the regular baseball season, Chicago found itself in an unaccustomed place: in a three-way tie for first!

Manager Joe Walsh walked through his team's locker room and tried to pump up each player individually. Glen sat at his locker smiling. *How could anyone need to be motivated for a game like this,* he wondered? *This is what it's all about.* When he finished buttoning his jersey, he ran his fingers across the navy blue and scarlet tackle twill lettering on the front. He traced the outline of the word Sox.

I wonder how those other Sox are gonna do today, he thought. *Wouldn't that be something to meet up with DT in the ALCS.* The White Sox' final game was against the Oakland Athletics. As defending American League champions, Oakland would not go down without a fight. The schedule had been kind to Chicago, though. The game was at Comiskey Park, and the A's had been on the road for eight days.

The hustling, hard-working character of the Sox was a natural extension of Scrapper. They contrasted sharply with the long ball hitting, offensive minded A's. Everyone knew there would be runs scored in this game. But he figured some defensive play would be the difference.

Late afternoon sun peaked through the clouds in Chicago as the game went into the fifth inning all tied up at 5-5. Chicago had its runs with singles, doubles, walks, and stolen bases. Oakland's five runs came on a two-run homer and a three-run homer.

When Oakland started its half of the sixth with another base hit, Glen nervously paced the area around second.

"We've gotta keep guys off base," he muttered as he picked up a small pebble and hucked it off the playing field. "They're gonna get their dingers. We've just got to keep them from killing us!"

Oakland's next two batters hit the first pitches they got for clean singles. Joe Walsh immediately came flying out of the Sox dugout. A conference at the mound followed. "What's the problem, Harris?" Walsh asked his pitcher Mort Harris.

"Nothing, Coach. Those were all good pitches. They're just getting lucky."

Walsh looked at his catcher. "Well, how's his stuff?"

Brian Freeman, the burly Sox backstop, shrugged. "Don't look at me, Coach. I haven't been catching them. They've been hitting them."

Glen suppressed a laugh. The tension of the moment seemed broken by the brutal honesty of his remark.

Walsh turned back to Harris. "Listen, Ace. Bounce a few up to the plate or something, will ya? We've gotta break this string up somehow."

Glen swatted Harris on the rear with his glove as he headed back toward second. "You can do it, Harris. Keep 'em low so we can get the double play somewhere."

"You heard the coach. I'll keep 'em plenty low."

The very next pitch was a sinker. The batter went down and dug it out and dribbled a grounder up the middle. Glen charged the ball and scooped it barehanded. After a split-second decision, he fired straight forward toward home.

The ball and the runner reached the plate at the same instant. Freeman was bowled over by the impact but held onto the ball. The umpire's hand flashed up as he screamed out the call. "OUT!"

Freeman struggled to his feet, then fired the ball back to his pitcher. He signaled the trainer that he was all right and adjusted his mask before squatting down behind the plate again. Fired up by the gutsy play, the Sox fielders became more animated and vocal.

"One down . . . one down. Let's look for the two," hollered Finnigan.

"Still a force at home," reminded Tyler Andressen, the third baseman.

Glen turned and held up one finger for the outfielders. This was standard procedure to make sure everyone knew what was going on.

Relieved to finally get an out, Harris started throwing with confidence again. He struck out the next batter and then got Oakland's big home-run threat, Tommy Davis, to pop out. The Sox had escaped a potential disaster.

Charged up, they came to the plate ready for action. Freeman started off the inning with a double. A walk, a single, and another double gave Chicago a two-run lead. Glen came to the plate next.

Okay, Mitchell, he told himself. *Now's the time to ice this sucker.* The fans tasted victory and were hungry for the finish. "C'mon Scrapper," they screamed.

"Knock one outta here!"

"Keep it going . . . keep it going!" Oakland's pitcher nervously eyed him.

"Give me something good," Glen said to himself as he watched the windup and the pitch.

When the ball came streaking down toward the middle of the plate, Glen couldn't believe his eyes. He coiled up like a spring and lashed at the pitch with his accurate swing.

Cheers rose from the fans as they jumped to their feet. The ball was zipping out toward the left field wall. It crashed against the fence and bounded back toward the infield. By the time the Oakland left fielder had retrieved the ball, Glen stood on second with a double and two more Chicago runners had crossed the plate.

"Wayda go, Mitchell!"

"Good stroke, Scraps!" his teammates screamed out.

Glen turned for a quick look at the scoreboard. When he saw the Oakland outfielders stumbling head down toward their positions he knew it was over. Chicago was up, 9-5. The game and the Western Division championships were theirs for the taking.

When Oakland failed to get anything going in the next two innings, Chicago started a wild celebration. Fans spilled out onto the field and started pulling up anything they could for souvenirs. It was the Sox' first trip to the play offs in more than ten years. The Chicago locker room was mayhem after the game. Reporters, hungry for a story, swarmed over the players and coaches. Glen found himself surrounded by a dozen microphones as he struggled to change out of his uniform.

"As a rookie, how does it feel to make the play offs in your first year?" one reporter asked.

"Great!" said Glen, laughing.

"Are you surprised at the team's success?"

"I'm used to being on a winner," Glen boasted. "I don't know what happened here before. That's all in the past. I'm only concerned with what we do now."

The recorders and cameras captured every word as he spoke.

The reporters continued their questions.

"Do the Sox have any preference on who they play in the championships?"

"I can't speak for the whole team," said Glen. "I don't think that anyone else has thought much past getting into the play offs."

"That sounds like you have. Who's your choice?" the reporter asked, trying to pin him down.

A thin smile formed across Glen's face. "Well . . . I've been following my old high school buddies pretty closely. . . . "

A reporter popped up from the back of the crowd. "David Green and Roberto Ramirez."

"Right," said Glen. The woman stepped forward and said, "I came out to your house the day you three were drafted out of Rosemont. It's been quite a story that all three of you have made it to the majors . . . and made it so quickly."

Glen wasn't one for false modesty. He nodded and said, "We all knew we could do it."

The reporter, Sarah Dixon, smiled at Glen. "I had a feeling you would, too."

Glen's eyes met hers and they moved no farther. Other reporters continued to ask questions, but it now became a conversation between Glen and Sarah.

She felt a blush on her cheek as they continued to stare at each other. Glancing down at her notepad, she said, "So I take it you want to play the Boston Red Sox in the play offs?"

"You got it. It'd be great to meet up with DT again. I think it'd be a heckuva series. How're they doing today anyway? Any score on their game?"

"They were behind in the fifth, I believe," Sarah said. "That's the last score I saw. But tell me, who would win if it was you two?"

"Is there any question about that?" Scrapper said, as he shrugged his shoulders.

The senior baseball reporter for the *Chicago Tribune* broke in. "So you're predicting a win for us in the LCS, right?" Feeling cocky and trying to impress the woman he was watching, Glen puffed up his chest and said, "I practically guarantee it!"

All the reporters frantically started scribbling down their notes. The television reporter turned to his cameraman and said, "Did you get that?"

A thumbs-up sign assured him he did.

By the time the crowd around him rushed off to file their stories, Glen knew that he might have made a mistake. Only Sarah remained behind to talk to him.

"I think I goofed, didn't I?" he said.

Sarah broke into an engaging laugh. "Let's just say that I have a pretty good idea what the lead-in sports story is going to be tonight."

Glen sank down onto the bench in front of his locker. "I'm cooked. Coach Walsh is gonna blow a gasket over this one. I just know it."

Placing a hand on his shoulder, Sarah tried to comfort him. "Don't worry about it too much. I'm sure he knows that players say things they don't mean to sometimes."

"That's not gonna cut it with him where I'm concerned. He and I have already had a run in or two about things I've said. He's not gonna like this one bit."

"Do you want me to talk to him?"

"No way!" Glen scoffed. "I don't want a woman to fight my battles for me. What do . . . "

Obviously upset, Sarah backed away. "I didn't mean it that way. I was only trying to help."

As she turned to leave the clubhouse, Glen jumped up and grabbed her arm. She spun around and faced him.

"I'm sorry," Glen said. "I'm having a heck 'uva time shooting my mouth off today. Can you forgive me?"

The frown on her face slowly gave way to her magical smile. The sparkle in her eyes returned, captivating Glen with its magnetic appeal.

"I'll try," she responded.

"Let me show you I mean it," Glen said. He fought back the increased beating in his heart and struggled to breathe normally. He worked up the courage to say, "Can I take you out to dinner tonight?"

Surprised, but pleased, Sarah nodded her head. "I think I'd like that very much."

Glen beamed. "Great. Where should I pick you up? What time would be good for you?"

She scribbled an address down on her notepad, tore the page off, and handed it to Glen. "You name the time."

"Seven?"

"I'll be ready," she said. When she turned and left the clubhouse, Glen couldn't take his eyes off of her.

For a minute, Glen forgot about everything else. The Western Division crown, a possible

series against David, and even his quote to the
press all faded from memory. For the next few
hours, all he could think about was Sarah
Dixon.

SEVEN

Roberto Ramirez squinted against the afternoon sun in Los Angeles. The Dodgers' final game of the season was a minor tune-up before their Championship Series against the St. Louis Cardinals.

Since Magic wasn't scheduled to pitch, he spent most of the day with his eyes glued to the big scoreboard out in center field. With the three-hour time difference between east coast and west, he knew the Boston game should be over pretty soon.

It's too much to ask for, he thought to himself as he checked the scores. *I should have known better.* He was lamenting the fact that Boston was behind in the late innings and Chicago started off its game by giving up two runs in the first. It didn't look good for either of his two friends making it into the play offs.

Going into that final day of the season, Roberto knew that if both David's and Glen's teams won, he'd be assured of meeting up against one of them if the Dodgers made it to the World Series.

When the Dodgers started a rally in its game against Houston, Roberto forgot about the scoreboard. The next time he remembered to look up, he was shocked at what he saw. "Holy smoke!" he screamed as he jumped up from the bench.

His teammates, startled by the unexplained outburst, just looked at him.

"Boston won!" he hollered.

A couple of Magic's friends on the team knew what he was excited about; the rest just thought he was nuts.

When the final score of the White Sox game got posted, Roberto was dancing up and down the dugout floor. "Yowwwwwsser, Yowwwwwsser, Yowwwwwwwwsser!" he bellowed. "They're in! They made it!"

When he quieted down and sat back on the bench he punched the air with his fist and said, "Now we've *got* to do it. We've got to make it to the World Series!"

David Green flipped on the TV when he woke up. He had been partying with his teammates until late last night, and it was hard to get up out of bed. He was searching for the headline news channel to catch the sports update. He still didn't know who had won the Western Division.

When the scores finally rolled across the screen David jumped up out of bed and flung his pillow at the TV.

"All right!" he screamed as he rose with both fists in the air.

The phone rang just as he started to settle down. He immediately recognized the voice on the other end. "Wayda go, Scrapper! You made it!"

"Magic . . . hey, man . . . how're ya doing?"

"Just great, DT. Can you hang on a second? This is a conference call. Just hold on."

A moment of silence was quickly replaced with two voices coming at him.

"Hey, Green . . . what's happening?"

"Scraps . . . you dog, you. Good to hear from you. I see you guys snuck into the play offs against us."

Glen laughed. "We wanted a piece of you Red Sox real bad. We figured it'd be easy money and a sure trip to the World Series."

"In your dreams, Mitchell," said David. "We're gonna beat you guys like a drum."

"Talk's cheap, pal. We'll see what happens when we get you out on the field tomorrow night."

David groaned. "That's right. We're gonna have to travel first, aren't we?"

"You'd better believe it. But don't worry . . . it'll be your last road trip of the year," said Glen laughing.

"You just wait . . . "

Roberto broke into the argument. "Hey, could you guys cool it long enough for me to say something? Geez, you'd think it was tough to get into the LCS to hear you guys talk. I thought it was easy."

"Yeah, that's just because you guys don't have to play anybody tough . . . that's why." Scrapper pushed the needle in a little deeper. "I've been looking at some of your box scores, Magic. I wouldn't be getting too excited if I were you."

Offended, Roberto's back went up. "You're one to talk, Punch-and-Judy hitter. I eat your kind up for lunch. Three pitches is what you'd see. If we played you pathetic Sox, you'd get six trips. Three to the plate and three back to the dugout."

David started laughing. "All right you two. Now it's my turn to break it up. Let's just be thankful we all made it to the show and now to the play offs. It's been one heckuva year!"

"You said it," echoed Glen.

Roberto agreed. "It's hard to believe. I'm really looking forward to seeing you guys again . . . one way or the other. I know it's gonna be tough on one of us . . . maybe two . . . if we don't make it to the Series, but we can look forward to getting together back home in a few weeks."

"Yeah," said David. "Glen's got it easy being so close to home. I haven't seen my family for a long time."

"Me, either," echoed Roberto.

"Well, you'd better hope you don't for a while longer, you guys. There's still baseball to be played," said Scrapper.

"And home runs to hit," added David. "And strike outs to throw," said Roberto, laughing.

"When are you guys flying out?" Glen asked David.

"I've gotta check in with the club in a few minutes. Morgan told us we could celebrate last night, so we did, but we've gotta be ready tomorrow. I think we'll leave early this afternoon so we can take it easy this evening and be raring to go against you guys."

Roberto broke in. "I read this morning that Ross is out for the year. I take it you've got yourself a full time job out in center now?"

"Looks that way. I don't think that homer yesterday hurt me any."

"Funny . . . very funny," Glen sneered. "You get the pennant-clinching homer, Roberto nails down the title with a win for his team . . . and I've gotta worry about getting suspended if I . . ."

"Don't tell me your temper is still getting you in trouble?" asked David.

"Where've you been?" said Roberto, laughing. "Didn't you know that our buddy duked it out with his *own* teammate last week and got put on the shelf for a game?"

"Nope. But then, in Boston nobody really gives a rip about White Sox. Only Red. That story didn't make our papers."

"Our scouts brought back the story," Roberto said.

"Scouts? You guys have scouts watching the Chicago White Sox?" David couldn't believe it.

Glen filled him in. "Hey, man. The Dodgers clinched their title so long ago, their coaches didn't have anything better to do than go watch who they might meet in the Series."

"I don't remember seeing or hearing anything about Dodgers' scouts being at any of our games," David said.

"Weren't you listening?" Glen scolded. "I said, teams that have a chance of playing them in the World Series!"

"Funny! Very funny. We've got as much chance as you do. Probably more!"

"Howdya figure?"

"We've only gotta win one of the first two in Chicago. Then it's three straight at home . . . and there's no way you're gonna win any games in Boston."

"Get real! What's so tough about playing in Boston? That cheap home run derby ball park of yours is nothing."

"Power wins in Boston. You can hit all the singles you want, Scrapper. We're gonna be pounding out HRs. We'll bury you!"

"We'll see who's standing after this," shouted Glen.

"Hey, hold on you two," Roberto jumped in, trying to cool things down. "Let's not get into any of that stuff. Let's just be thankful that we've all been as fortunate as we've been . . . and be happy for each other's successes."

After a second's pause, David agreed. "Right on." Glen laughed. "Done!"

Roberto changed the subject. "So what else is new with you guys? Anything exciting going on . . . besides baseball?"

"I've been to some great parties," said David chuckling. "They'd put our old high school blasts to shame!"

"Some things don't change. Do they, Magic?" Glen asked.

"He's still the same, all right."Roberto said. "Always knows where the action is."

David said, "What's wrong with a little relaxation? It gets pretty boring living in hotel rooms, doesn't it?"

"Can't argue with that," Roberto said. "Just as long as you don't get yourself in any trouble."

"Trouble?" asked David.

"You know what I mean. There's been a lot of baseball players who've gotten mixed up with . . . "

"Don't even say it," yelled David. "You know me better than that. I'm not stupid. Drugs are for the ignorant. Sooner or later they'll screw up everything, and I'm not getting involved."

Roberto sighed in relief. "Good!"

David seemed compelled to cleanse himself. "I'm not saying I haven't seen them . . . some of my teammates might even be involved. But don't worry about me. I know it's a ticket to nowhere . . . usually one-way!"

"Right on," Magic firmly stated. David noticed it had been a two way conversation. "Glen? Why so quiet? Nothing bothering you, is there?"

Glen shook the daydream out of his head. "No . . . nothing . . . I was just thinking."

"'Bout what?" David asked.

"Nothing . . . really."

"What have you been doing to relieve those long, lonely hours by yourself?" asked DT.

The silence that followed, tipped off Roberto and David that something was up. Finally, Glen said, "I just go out with friends once in a while. Movies . . . dinner . . . that kinda thing."

"Okay, pal, what's the story?" David asked. "I can tell by the tone of your voice, you're covering something up!"

Roberto jumped in. "Whenever you get quiet, Scrapper, it's a dead giveaway something's going on."

"Well," Glen began, "I did have a great time last night with Sarah. . . . "

"Whoa! What have we here? Sarah? What's the skinny, Mitchell?" David was relentless.

"Hey. I just met her. She's a reporter with the *Tribune*. You guys both have seen her before."

"What? No way," said Magic.

"Oh yeah? Think back to the day we got drafted. At my house . . . all those reporters trying to question us." "Yeah," David mused. "I remember now. Blond girl, big blue eyes, short, but a real nice . . . "

"Don't say it," Glen warned.

" . . .personality," David said, laughing. "What the heck is she doing with you?"

"She likes me," bragged Scrapper.

"Or . . . she's looking for some kinda inside story," warned Roberto.

"Nah, she's not like that," Glen scoffed.

"Oh, you already know what she's like?" David said.

"Well enough to know she wouldn't have anything to do with knuckleheads like you. End of subject."

"Hey, Roberto," David shouted over the phone.

"Yeah."

"When we get back to Rosemont, we're gonna hafta look this chick up. Whadya say?"

"Absolutely. I'm way ahead of you on that one."

Glen became irate. "You guys just stay away from her . . . understand?"

"Ooh, definitely sounding serious, Mitchell. Sounding very serious," Roberto said, and laughed.

"Forget it, you chumps. We've only had one date. There's nothing there, so just drop it."

"We'll drop it all right for a while. We'll get back on it after the play offs," said David. "Count on it," added Roberto.

"Gee, with friends like you, who needs anyone else?" growled Glen.

"You're right!" said David. "But enough's enough. I've gotta get ready to go. I'm really glad you guys called."

"The pleasure was all Glen's," Roberto stated. "It's all on his dime. I charged it to him."

"I'm starting to wonder about you, Ramirez," grumbled Glen.

"Well, anyway . . . good luck in the play offs, Magic. I'll be rooting for you," David said.

"Thanks, pal. And good luck to both of you against each other."

"Luck won't have anything to do with it," said Glen. "We're gonna teach those long ball hitters some fundamentals!"

"We'll see," David said calmly. "Okay, Magic. Thanks again for calling, and I'll see you in the Series in about a week, okay?"

"Whoever," said Magic. "I know one of you guys will be there. I hope I can join you."

David gave his friend some encouragement. "Don't worry about it. You'll do fine. Just relax and let it happen."

Thanks for the support. I'll talk to you both later."

David finished up. "See ya, Magic. And Glen?"

"Yeah?"

"I really hope you have a good series. No matter who wins I'm looking forward to seeing you again. Okay?"

"Thanks, DT. Same here. Now . . . it's off to the League Championship Series!"

"All right!" they all shouted as they hung up their phones.

EIGHT

The city of Chicago really came alive for the Sox. It had been eight years since their last trip to the play offs. It was twenty-nine years since their last trip to the World Series, and the fans weren't going to miss this opportunity to root for their home team.

When Glen arrived at the stadium for the first game of the LCS, he was surprised at how different everything looked. The field had been meticulously manicured and chalked with special colors and designs. Banners and bunting hung from every fa₈ade. Filled to capacity for the first time in years, the old stadium seemed alive with a special energy.

"Boy, this is really something," he said to Finnigan as they stood out by second base.

"The play offs . . . a whole different season all right. It's great!" he said.

"I hope we're all ready for it," Glen wondered aloud. "This means a lot to me."

Finnigan scooped up a grounder and flipped it back toward first. "'Cause of your friend on the Red Sox."

"Yeah. I want to beat Green bad — for old time's sake."

The next practice grounder came bounding out to Glen. Effortlessly, he cradled the ball in his glove and fired the throw to first on a line.

"We all want to win, too. Only problem is, only one team will win," offered Finnigan.

"Yep. Where would the winners be without the losers?" joked Glen. "I just don't wanna be practicing to be a good loser. I'd rather try and be a gracious winner."

When warm-ups were over, both teams sat down in their dugouts. Each team was introduced, one by one, and the players came out and stood on their foul lines leading away from home plate. When everyone was out on the field, the crowd rose for the national anthem.

The first notes from the Marine marching band sent goose bumps down Scrapper's back. He remembered how he had felt when the Rosemont Rockets had squared off against East High for the Illinois state championship, just two years ago. There wasn't a feeling to describe the combination of exhilaration and nausea that swept over him.

Luckily, the upset stomach before big games always disappeared as soon as the action started. Playing ball was much easier than waiting. When he reached his spot at second base Glen quickly peered into the Boston dugout to find David. Their eyes met briefly and a grin crossed their faces.

Boston's lineup was truly amazing. From the lead off hitter, Jason Burke, all the way down to their Number Nine man, they were loaded with power. Each player was capable of deciding a game with one swing of the bat.

Chicago had gone over its game plan several times. Glen knew that if his pitchers kept the ball low and away from the Boston hitters, he would be seeing a lot of ground balls his way. "Just the way I like," he said to himself as he watched Burke dig in at the plate.

Just as they had diagrammed it, Burke took the first pitch and bounced an easy roller to Scrapper. He gobbled it up and flipped to first for the first out. The crowd immediately started cheering as if it were the final out of the World Series.

"Take it easy, guys," Glen said to the crowd as he looked around at the packed house. "We've got a long way to go. Don't burn out too early."

The next Boston player grounded out to Finnigan for the second out. Glen smiled. David Green was coming to the plate. "Okay, Jerry . . . blow it by him . . . this guy ain't nothing!" Glen yelled to his pitcher.

A broad grin appeared on David's face. He had heard his buddy out in the field.

"Hum it in there. Hum it in there," the infield chatter went.

The first pitch to DT bounced on the plate for ball one.

"A little higher, Jerry. You can do it. No problem!"

Jerry Norris, Chicago's best pitcher, decided to challenge the young rookie batter with a fastball. Glen watched the pitch and cringed when he saw where it was headed.

"Look out up there. Look out!" Glen screamed as he tried to distract his old teammate.

David wasn't fooled. He saw the pitch and his eyes lighted up. But he was surprised to see it, and in his anxiousness got out way ahead of it. His powerful swing caught the ball well in front of the plate. The tremendous clout took off toward the upper deck of Comiskey Stadium and went foul as it headed out of the park.

Glen yelled at the pitcher. "Hey, Norris, keep it down and away. This guy can hit," Glen shouted.

Norris was unshaken. "Let me do the pitching, Mitchell. This guy can't be so tough."

Glen shook his head. "Hey, Jerry," he said. "That was your fastball you just threw, wasn't it?"

The Chicago hurler got the point. It was his best pitch, and yet the batter had got out on it and had driven it with power. For a power pitcher, that was not a good sign.

"Okay, okay. I'll take care of it," he called back to his young infielder. "You be ready now if he hits it your way."

Just as if it were planned, Norris threw a low inside pitch to David and he smacked a hard grounder between second and first. Glen raced to his left, gloved the hot smash, and tossed it to first for the out. The crowd rose to their feet as the top half of the first ended, and gave their team a hand.

When David circled the bag and headed back for the dugout to get his hat and glove, he passed Glen. "Nice play, creep. I'll get it past you next time."

Chicago's batting order started off with Rick Finnigan and Glen Mitchell. Between the two of them, they had an on-base percentage of close to .500. A base hit was a great way to start a game.

But whether it was nerves, good pitching, or both, neither one could manage it, and the White Sox went down in order in their half of the first.

The game quickly settled into a defensive struggle. Exactly the kind of game that Chicago wanted. They weren't interested in trying to slug it out with the stronger Red Sox.

When they entered the top of the seventh, the score was still 0-0.

The first batter up for Boston was David Green. After grounding out in the first, he flew out to center in the fourth. It was one of the few balls hit out of the infield . . . by either team.

Chicago's infielders tried to keep their pitcher sharp.

"C'mon, Jerry! You can do it. This guy's nothing."

"Keep it going. Keep it going!"

Glen watched Norris peering in for the sign. He snuck a peek and edged toward second base, knowing a fastball was going in. It wouldn't be as likely that David would pull a fastball so Glen protected up the middle.

The pitcher wound up and delivered. The ball sailed from his hand and headed right for the batter's head. David spun around and down and just missed getting hit.

The Boston team had just stepped out of the dugout when they were called back by their manager. He was convinced that it had been an accident. There was no reason for Norris to be throwing at the unknown rookie.

Glen paced around the bag at second. He was thankful that his buddy wasn't hurt but nervous about what would happen next.

Norris shook off the catcher's signal for a curve. Nodding on the next sign, he started his windup. Glen had a sinking feeling in his stomach. It didn't last for long.

David stood at the plate with his eyes focused on the pitcher. When Norris's fastball came streaking in toward the outside corner of the plate he was ready.

The thick part of the bat caught the ball flush. The horsehide sphere rebounded off the flame-treated ash like a superball off of concrete. Norris spun around as quickly as he could but still didn't pick up the flight of the ball.

Glen slammed his glove against his left thigh. He didn't have to look to find the ball. He knew it was headed out of the park.

David started into his home-run trot as soon as he dropped his bat. Then as he circled first and headed for second, David stole a glance at his friend and gave him a thumbs-up sign.

Glen nodded quickly and looked to the ground. Under his breath he said, "I told the jerk not to give you anything."

"Glad he doesn't listen well," David said as he headed on his way.

The ball came down forty rows deep in straightaway center field. It had to have traveled at least 375 feet. The crowd sat silently as David crossed home plate with the game's first run. Norris stomped around the mound and stared several times at his rookie second baseman. It was as if he somehow blamed Glen for David's home run.

The rest of the game went just as the beginning had. When Chicago went down in order in the bottom of the ninth, the final score still read 1-0.

Boston's team celebrated wildly in its dugout. Chicago's team sank slowly into the bow-
els of the stadium, seeking the solitude of its
locker room.

Roberto Ramirez struggled to control his
nerves. He wasn't even pitching the first game
of the National League championships, but he
felt just as bad. He kept walking to the water
cooler, desperately trying to shake the butter-
flies in his stomach.

*Geez, what's it gonna be like when I hafta go
out on the mound?* he thought to himself.

The Dodgers were at home for the opener
against the St. Louis Cardinals. The Cards had
overcome a five game lead held by the New
York Mets to win the Eastern Division race.
Playing them was going to be like facing a
mirror. Both teams relied on pitching, speed,
and defense. This series would certainly be decided by the team that could best stick to its
game plan.

Roberto already knew that Boston was one
game up in its series with Chicago. He was
proud that David had hit the game-winning
homer. Scrapper was probably steaming mad.

Left to sit and watch from the bench, Roberto
struggled with his anxiety throughout the
game. Without the action to help take his mind
off the pressure, he could do nothing but worry
about what was happening.

Luckily, the Dodgers eeked out the first score of the game in the second inning. A hit batsman, a stolen base, a sacrifice, and a fielder's choice produced a hitless run.

Roberto thought for a while that one run might be enough, at least the way Enrico Valesquez was pitching, it seemed like enough. The Dodgers' crafty veteran had scattered seven hits through seven innings and held St. Louis scoreless.

But when the Cards put together a rally of its own in the eighth, Roberto saw the scoreboard change to 3-1 St. Louis. The way his teammates had been hitting, Roberto felt like it was curtains.

With two out in the ninth, a walk to Davey Smith kept L.A.'s hopes alive. When the next batter singled, the fans started chanting and stomping their feet.

Knowing he was supposed to pitch the next game, Roberto was hoping and praying for a rally. He didn't want to face the Cards with his team already down by one game.

Steve Henderson came to the plate. The only Dodger who could be considered a long ball threat dug in at the plate with one thing in mind. Waiting patiently for his pitch, he saw the count go to 3 and 1.

Confident the next pitch would be a fastball, Henderson bore down on the end of his bat and tensed his massive forearms.

Sure enough, the fastball came in. Henderson caught it squarely and sent a long fly ball toward the wall. But unfortunately for L.A., he didn't pull it enough. Hit toward straight away center, the long drive was swallowed up by Dodger Stadium's massive center field. The Cards center fielder raced to the warning track and made the catch.

Erupting in cheers, St. Louis raced off the field and headed for its clubhouse to enjoy the victory. The Dodgers trotted off with their heads down.

Valesquez walked to the clubhouse next to Roberto, who slapped him on the back. "You pitched great, man. Too bad we couldn't get you any runs."

"That's baseball, kid. If you let it, it could drive you nuts. How many times have you gone out there and thrown a shutout when your team scores seven or eight runs and then when you give up one or two, they go scoreless. Who can figure it?"

"Pitching is a tough job," Roberto said.

Valesquez put his glove on Roberto's head. "Hey, it's up to you tomorrow, kid. Good luck."

Roberto felt the pit of his stomach roll over again. "Thanks. I'm gonna need it!"

NINE

Roberto raced to Dodger Stadium as soon as he woke up. He had spent a sleepless night tossing and turning, worrying about his start against the St. Louis Cardinals. With one loss already, he knew that everything rode on this game for his teammates. Going to St. Louis down by two games would certainly be fatal.

It was five o'clock in the morning the last time Roberto looked at his watch. He finally fell asleep from extreme nervous exhaustion. The next time he saw his clock, it was eleven-thirty.

"The coach is gonna kill me," Magic decided as he raced through the parking lot and headed for the clubhouse. "I should have been here an hour ago."

The Dodgers were forced to play the afternoon game that day because of television scheduling. The Chicago—Boston game was to be shown in prime time in the East, so L.A. and St. Louis got an early start. At least they'd get an early flight out that night so they could be in Missouri tomorrow, Roberto thought.

"Ramirez, glad you could join us," Dave Westrum yelled as his rookie entered the locker.

"Sorry, Coach. I couldn't get to sleep last night."

"I'm not gonna ask how that makes sense, Ramirez. Just tell me you're ready to go!"

"No problem," Magic anxiously responded.

"Step on it, then. I presume you might still need to warm up a little before the game, which by the way starts in forty minutes! You'd better get a move on it."

"On my way."

Roberto tossed his uniform on in record time. He didn't put on his baseball undershirt, though. The temperature was already eighty-five and he didn't think he'd need it.

When Roberto got to the bullpen, he started slowly tossing the ball back and forth to the bullpen catcher, Steve Henderson. Each throw was just a little harder until finally, after about twenty pitches, his velocity was up to full speed.

"Looking good, Magic," Henderson said.

"Yeah, I feel real strong for some reason. I hope that's a good sign."

"It's gotta be better than feeling lousy. Anyway, we'd better head into the dugout. They're

gonna be introducing the starting lineups pretty soon."

Magic nodded and made one last toss. The
ball exploded into the catchers' glove with a
loud pop.

"Whew! Smokin' there, Ramirez," Henderson
said. "Those guys are gonna be swinging at air
today!"

"Yeah, I hope so."

The announcer's voice echoed through the
vast reaches of Dodger Stadium. "Good afternoon, ladies and gentlemen. Welcome to the
second game of the League Championship Series between the St. Louis Cardinals . . . " Scattered boos filled the park, " . . .and your Los
Angeles Dodgers!" Cheers drowned out the last
two words.

After the player introductions, Roberto trotted out to the mound with the rest of his team.
He anxiously paced around the small circular
patch of dirt. Finding the rosin bag, he moved it
to a spot behind and to the left of him, a super-
stition he had always followed.

He took his warm up tosses and struggled to
control the burning sensation in his stomach.
Licking his lips, he leaned forward, glove hand
on his knee, and took his sign from the catcher.

"Here goes," he sighed as he started his
windup.

The first pitch ripped in, right down the middle.

"Striiiike!" yelled the umpire.

The fans in Dodger Stadium let out a raucous cheer. They all knew how important this game was.

When Roberto's next two pitches sailed wide of the plate the crowd noise started to lower. The third ball made everyone very restless.

The Dodgers catcher stood up and motioned to Magic to calm down. He could see his starter struggling with his tempo and his delivery. He didn't want him to get off to a bad start.

His first four pitches had done nothing to relieve Roberto's nervousness. He pushed his cap back on his head and wiped the sweat from his brow. He took another deep breath and tried to kick himself into gear.

"C'mon, don't do this to yourself. Relax and fire!" he grumbled.

Going with his bread-and-butter pitch, the split-fingered fastball, Roberto was relieved when the batter swung for a second strike. Given another chance, he came back with his heat and blew the ball by the batter.

"Striiiike Threeeeeee!" was the call.

Roberto felt as though the weight of the world had been lifted from his shoulders. He had got by that first out — always his toughest. The next two batters were no problem. An easy grounder to short and another strikeout ended the inning.

"Looking good, kid," Lasorda said as Magic dropped down on the bench to relax.

"Thanks, Coach. I feel pretty good now."

"Try to hold on to it."

For the next four innings, he did. Batter after batter came to the plate for the Cardinals, but none of them found the secret to hitting Magic. Fifteen batters had come up so far and fifteen batters had gone down.

But the Dodgers had almost the same luck with the St. Louis pitcher. Other than a few scratch singles, they had had little luck and no runs. At the end of five complete innings the score remained as it had started, 0-0.

Henderson walked out toward the field with Roberto at the start of the sixth inning. It was still early, but the thought of a no-hitter was starting to cross his mind. He hoped it wasn't on Roberto's.

"Remember, kid," he warned, "if there's a runner on second we'll go to the "C" series of signs so he can't pick them up."

"Right," Magic nodded.

"And one more thing . . . keep alert for bunts. They're gonna start trying anything they can to get on, since they haven't had much luck getting around on your fastball."

"Gotcha," Roberto said, and winked. "I'll cover the lines and try to pounce on anything they get down."

Henderson walked toward the plate and pulled his mask down over his face. "One more thing," he yelled. "Keep that left foot pointing toward home when you plant it. It's when you get a little sideways that the ball starts sailing on you."

"Good point. I'll stay on top of it," Roberto hollered back.

But the effort to keep him loose and ready was unnecessary. Once Roberto got past the start of the inning he was in complete control of his pitching. His breaking ball was cracking. His fastball was really popping, and his confidence was strong.

As quickly as the Cardinals marched to the plate in the sixth, Roberto sent them marching back to the dugout. Three up and three down.

When the first L.A. batter got a base on balls, Roberto went to the plate with one thing in mind: sacrifice.

He stepped into the batter's box, looked down at "Cookie" Lohenzotta, the third base coach, and got his sign.

No surprise there, Magic thought, smiling to himself. *I don't suppose it'll be a surprise to anyone in the park!* Sure enough, when he squared around to lay down a bunt the Cardinals third and first basemen were right on top of him, waiting.

Hoping to get a pop up, the Cards hurler threw his pitch high. Roberto was smart enough to lay off. He knew how hard it was to get a bunt down on a high pitch.

"I'll wait for something a little better," he said to the catcher with a smile.

"You might not get one," the Cards backstop said, laughing.

The next pitch came in a little high too, but the umpire called it a strike. The count evened at 1-1.

"Look alive. Look alive," the St. Louis coaches yelled from the dugout.

Roberto glanced down toward Cookie again. Surprised, he stepped out of the box. He got the hit-away sign.

He checked the series of hand motions and signals and stepped back into the box. When the pitcher started his windup the Cardinal infielders started their dash toward home.

Instead of squaring around to bunt, though, Roberto slapped at the outside fastball and sent a line drive right at the charging first baseman. It was all he could do to get a glove up and protect his face. He managed to knock the ball down but it bounded away from him, and Roberto easily scampered on to first.

Now there were runners at first and second with nobody out rather than a runner at second with one away. The call by the Dodgers' brain trust had been a good one.

Roberto beamed as he stood on the bag at first. He was always thrilled when he was able to contribute with his bat. As he had been a pretty fair hitter in high school, it irritated him that no one in professional ball thought much about a pitcher's hitting ability.

"Maybe that'll help show 'em," he said to the first base coach while waiting for the next batter, "we pitchers can hit too!"

With the Dodgers top of the order coming to the plate, the fans started stomping their feet. A rally was definitely in order.

But the excitement was dampened when the lead off hitter grounded out to third, forcing the runner coming down, and the next batter struck out. Roberto's surprise hit became very important, though. Mark Brown rapped a single down the right-field line, and the runner on second scampered all the way home to give the Dodgers a 1-0 lead. And the way Roberto was pitching, it was looking better for L.A.

The rally ended with just one run, and the Dodgers ran out onto the field to try to make it stand up. The seventh inning continued perfect for Roberto and a struggle for the Dodgers. Entering the eighth, L.A. still had a slim one-run lead.

The first batter for St. Louis in the top of the eighth was its clean-up hitter, Boog Moore. A mountain of a man at over six feet seven and 260 pounds, he looked like he should be a tackle on a football team. But his immense size distracted people from his respectable speed and great coordination. He was truly an all around athlete.

Roberto had kept the ball well away from him his first two at bats. This time, the game plan was to jam him inside. Henderson set up

with his glove on the inside corner and signaled for the fastball.

Magic wound up and threw. Boog had read
their minds.

His bat connected solidly. Roberto's face con-
torted into a grimace as he heard the impact of
horsehide on ash. He didn't have to look to see
the results. In an instant, the ball was rico-
cheting off the top of the scoreboard in center
field. Boog went into his best home run trot.
The no-hitter, perfect game, shutout, and one-
run lead had vanished with one swing of the
bat.

Roberto kicked at the pitcher's rubber and
cursed his stupidity. *Why did I try to throw him
inside? We got him out twice pitching him inside. How dumb can we be?* Henderson went
out to the mound. "My fault, kid. I shouldn't
have called that pitch."

Roberto shook his head. "I threw it, you
didn't. If it would have been faster or lower or
more inside, he couldn't have done that. It was
just a mistake."

Happy that his pitcher had a good attitude,
Henderson slapped him on the back and headed back behind the plate. "Let's forget it. Just
get these next three batters and we'll get that
run back!"

Roberto did his part. Angry after his gopher-
ball pitch, his next nine pitches had a little
more heat than normal on them. He struck out
all three batters who came up.

In their half of the eighth, the Dodgers went down weakly. It seemed the momentum of the game was up for grabs. Boog's homer had lifted St. Louis's spirits and dampened L.A.'s.

Roberto was still strong in the ninth. The first two batters were easy outs. The third one, Jerome Davis, wasn't. He hit a chopper right up the middle that bounced over Roberto's head and into center field.

The crowd grew restless, but only for an instant. Bearing down again and reaching for that little extra reserve of strength, he struck out the next batter to end the threat.

The Dodgers came up in the bottom of the ninth with a chance to end it right there.

"C'mon you guys," Lasorda yelled. "Let's do it!"

"We need something right now," Henderson echoed.

Magic clapped his hands and tried to fire up his teammates. "Only one . . . we only need one!"

The first Dodger batter worked the count carefully and drew a walk. The crowd's decibel level started rising. But the next two batters hit ground balls to the infield for two outs. Roberto moved up to the on-deck circle. If "Foots" Walters could get on base, Magic would get to bat.

Walters took the first pitch he saw and rapped it into left field. Off with the hit, the runner on first made it all the way to third on a daring bit of base running. Immediately, the fans were on their feet screaming for more.

Roberto took two steps toward the plate, but was called back by Lasorda. Roberto turned around and saw Reese McCoy grab two bats and step out of the dugout. They were putting in a pinch hitter for him.

He walked over to the dugout and sat next to Henderson. "They do this to me," Roberto groaned.

"No big deal, kid. They got to play the percentages, kid. Reese is a lefty and a better hitter than you. We only need one hit here and it's over. You've done your job today. You pitched super. Give it a rest!"

Roberto sank down into the dugout and watched. He knew if McCoy got a hit, he'd be the winning pitcher. If not, it would be a no decision game for him.

McCoy popped out.

The Dodgers grabbed their gloves and headed back onto the field. Except for Magic. All he could do now was watch. His team's spirits had sunk dramatically. Now he was worried they were going to lose.

"C'mon you guys. Fire up out there! We can do it. We can do it!" he yelled.

The rookie's words seemed to help the veteran team. They held the Cards scoreless again in the top of the tenth. The players ran in from the field with their fists in the air.

"Now's the time," they screamed.

"C'mon everybody, we can't let this get away."

"This game is ours!"

And, two batters later it was. A double followed by a single up the middle was all it took. When Mark Brown hit the plate with the winning run, the team charged out of the dugout and the fans erupted in wild cheers.

"We did it!"

"Great win, guys," Lasorda yelled as he led the troops back toward the clubhouse.

A little upset he didn't get the win, Roberto still found satisfaction in his performance. He felt even better when Lasorda called his players together in the locker room for a talk.

"You guys did great today. That was one heckuva ball game. You all showed a lot of character out there. I'm proud of ya!"

The locker room exploded in cheers.

Lasorda held up one hand. "And I think we ought to give a special cheer to one of the great pitching performances I've ever seen in the play offs. Only one mistake the whole game. C'mon you guys, lets hear it for our ace rookie. Stand up, Ramirez!"

The room erupted. Magic's broad smile was covered by a hundred towels and jerseys being thrown at him. But he didn't mind. That day had just become one of the happiest of his life.

TEN

"Hey, Mitchell . . . your socks don't match!"

David sat on the dugout bench in Chicago and watched his opponents, the White Sox, take batting practice. He enjoyed watching his buddy Glen Mitchell, and couldn't resist heckling him now that he had the chance.

With a one-game lead in the best-of-seven League Championship Series, Boston was relaxed, loose, and happy. Another win in Chicago would be icing on the cake.

Scrapper almost looked down but stopped himself just in time. His lips curled upward in a smile. He glanced over at his manager, who was watching from the top step of the Chicago dugout, and decided against answering his friends' taunts.

The first pitch came in and Glen rapped it sharply into left field. He knew that would get David's attention.

"If those fences were in about fifty feet," David called out, "that guy might become a factor!"

Mitchell got ready for the next pitch.

"C'mon, pitcher. Groove one for him. Let's see if he can get one out of this shoe box!" David yelled.

The entire Chicago team stopped what they were doing to watch and listen to the show. Most of them knew who was yelling from the Boston sidelines, and why. They loved to see Mitchell get some of his mouth back for a change.

Scrapper dug in with his cleats, seeking that extra power for the next pitch. When he saw it coming straight down the middle, he let himself go. With a ferocious cut, he got under the ball and lifted a high fly ball toward the outfield wall.

His teammates started clapping as they saw the height and length of the smash. They were sure it was a homer. Glen didn't move. The hard cut had spun him around with his weight on his left side. Silently he cheered on the ball as it flew over the fence.

"That'll do it," Mitchell yelled. "That other team hasn't got anybody out there who can catch those."

David was about to reply when he saw his manager emerge from the clubhouse hallway into the dugout. He sat back on the bench without answering Scrapper's insult.

"Green," said Morgan. "I think you've seen enough out here. We're gonna have a team meeting in the locker room now. Let's go."

"Sure, Coach. I was just checking out the competition."

"I have a pretty good idea of what you were doing, Green. Let's forget it for now and concentrate on the game tonight. If we can win this one, there'll be plenty of time for heckling."

David smiled as Morgan winked at him. "Right, Coach."

The sun was just setting in Chicago when the band fired up its rendition of the national anthem. Scrapper was standing on the first base foul line, David on the third base line. As they looked out toward the flag, rippling in the breeze out in center field, they glanced back and forth at each other.

When the call came to play ball they nodded toward one another and ran toward their respective dugouts. It was time to forget about friendships and concentrate on winning.

DT and Scrapper both knew that Roberto's Dodgers had won its afternoon game. The thought of meeting up with him in the World Series was on both of their minds.

Chicago took the field, and David moved down the bench looking for his favorite thirty-six—ounce bat. Due up third in the inning, he was anxious to get things going.

The first two Red Sox batters both flied out. Carl Wolk, Chicago's sinker-ball specialist, seemed to be in fine form. David knew he wouldn't see anything above his shins so he decided to be patient and wait for a mistake. When it didn't happen, he took his base on balls, all four pitches low.

The next batter immediately bounced the ball to second. Scrapper scooped it up and trotted to second to tag the bag. David was forced out and the inning was over.

As he turned toward the Chicago dugout, Scrapper flipped the ball to David.

"Here, you can give this to your pitcher. You're headed that way."

The White Sox lead off hitter drew a walk, so Scrapper came to the plate with the crowd roaring for action. He dug his foothold in the batter's box and then looked down for the sign from his third-base coach.

"Good call," he mumbled under his breath. "The hit-and-run should get things going for us!"

Chicago's game plan was for the runner to break with the pitch. When the shortstop or second baseman moved over to cover the bag at second Glen was to try and hit it into the hole created by the move. Known for his excellent bat control, Scrapper was the perfect batter for the hit-and-run.

The pitch came in to Scrapper on the outside corner of the plate. Finnigan had taken off from first and was already two thirds of the way to second. Glen saw that the second baseman was covering the bag for some strange reason, so he tried to slap the ball toward right field.

It couldn't have been drawn up better. The Red Sox second baseman was caught running toward the bag and couldn't reverse direction fast enough to get to Scrapper's grounder. It took a high hop into right center, and Finnigan rounded the bag and headed for third.

David, playing shallow, raced in for the ball. He and the right fielder got to it at the same time, but David waved him off. Grabbing the ball with his bare hand, David came up throwing and gunned the ball toward third.

"Hit the dirt! Hit the dirt!" the third-base coach screamed.

Finnigan knew it was going to be close. Diving headfirst he reached for the bag with his outstretched hand. His fingers scrambled for the bag, but all they found was the waiting glove, ball in the hand, of the White Sox's third baseman.

"You're outta there!" the umpire called as his thumb rose through the air.

David's throw had been perfect. Finnigan never really had a chance against the line shot that one-hopped directly into the base.

The third baseman came up firing. He whipped the ball to second to prevent Glen from taking the extra base. Halfway between first and second, he had to turn and scramble back to first to avoid the putout.

"Great throw, Green!" his teammates yelled out to David.

"Heads up play!"

David nodded to his fellow Red Sox and returned to his position out in center. He thought about turning to check out Glen but decided against it.

"I *knew* I shouldn't have hit it out to center," Glen grumbled as he slapped his own thigh. "That was stupid! I won't let that happen again!"

The next two White Sox both popped out and the start of a rally died as quickly as it had begun. After one complete inning the score was 0-0.

The game moved rapidly through the early innings, as neither team could score. After four innings there was still no score.

In the bottom of the fifth, Scrapper led off the inning against Chip "Fireball" Reed. Getting the pitch he was looking for, Glen smashed a line shot into left field for a single.

"Good start, good start! Let's keep it going, guys!" the players yelled from the bench.

Scrapper knew that his team needed something to fire it up. He edged off the bag as far as he dared and rocked back and forth on the balls of his feet.

Reed kept a careful eye on him. After several throws to first to keep Glen close, he finally hurried a fastball to the plate. It was outside for a ball.

Another rushed throw to the batter produced another ball. Glen's antics on first were bugging Boston's pitcher. His strategy was working. But when the next two pitches caught corners of the plate for strikes, Scrapper decided to take things a step further. As soon as Reed's leg started toward home, he took off for second.

Hurrying to get the throw off, Boston's catcher had trouble digging the ball out of his glove. He then overthrew trying to get more speed on the ball. It bounced well short of second and skipped past the second baseman.

Scrapper's slide had barely started before he bounced up again and rounded the bag. Never hesitating, he dug four steps toward third before he remembered who was out in center.

"Oh, my God!" he grimaced. "I'm dead meat!"

Slamming on his brakes, he screeched to a halt and turned back toward second base. Not knowing where the throw was going, he took a couple of stumbling steps and then dove headfirst into second.

He felt the glove of the second baseman come slamming down on his head just as his fingers found the bag.

Whew! he thought to himself. *I made it.* "You're *Out!*" bellowed the umpire's voice.

"What?" Scrapper screamed. "You're outta your mind!"

Jumping up to his feet, Scrapper tore over to the umpire and stuck his face right up next to his. "How could you be so damn blind? That was the worst call I've ever seen!"

"Watch it, Mitchell," the umpire warned.

"Man, that wasn't even close. Who the hell were you watching up in the stands to miss that? Get in the ball game, will ya?"

The umpire turned away and walked back to his position. Scrapper was right in his footsteps.

Chicago's manager raced out to argue the call. He pulled Glen away from the umpire and pushed him toward the dugout.

"I'll handle this, Mitchell!"

But Scrapper was out of control. He circled around and got back in the face of the umpire. His teammates could see the end was near and ran over to pull him away.

"You can't make a bonehead call like that in an important game!" Scrapper screamed. "Who's paying . . . "

Finnigan slapped his hand over Scrapper's mouth. He knew that an umpire will not accept certain insults or assaults on his integrity. Wrestling his teammate to the ground, Finnigan started worrying about his own safety.

"Let me up," Scrapper yelled. "Let me at him!"

"You can't get yourself thrown outta here, Mitchell," Finnigan pleaded. "Get ahold of yourself!"

Finnigan refused to loosen his headlock. The struggle continued for several seconds until finally Glen started to calm down. Finally, his body went limp. "Okay, you can let go of me. I'm okay," he said.

The White Sox shortstop slowly let go of his teammate.

"You okay?" he asked warily.

"Better," Scrapper said.

Order was restored, and his teammate and manager led Scrapper back to the bench. The stadium crowd was on its feet, cheering for Glen and screaming for the umpire's head.

The electricity in the air seemed to supercharge the White Sox. On the very next pitch, the Chicago batter rammed a base hit up the middle. This was quickly followed by a another single, then a triple that scored two runs. Then, another single. The Chisox were up 3-0.

Reed, the Boston starter, was relieved. His sub fared no better. A single, a walk, and then a double brought in two more runs. The rally continued, and before he had even completely calmed down Glen found himself in the on deck circle, next up to the plate. With the score now at 5-0, there were two outs and the bases were loaded.

David was going nuts. Pacing around in the outfield, he could barely stand watching what

was happening to his team. Since joining the
team, he had never witnessed them get blown
out of a game like this.

Glen scraped the last remnants of white
chalk off the back line of the batter's box. He
stared out at the pitcher and focused his concentration and energy on one thing. When the
white ball came floating up to the plate every
fiber of his body poured into the pitch.

David couldn't believe it. As soon as the ball
left the bat, he took off running. After a couple
of steps he slowed down.

"That no-good little jerk," he grumbled.

Glen took off running toward first. By the
time he hit the bag he leaped into the air and
started hopping and skipping toward second.
His fly ball cleared the wall in left field for a
grand slam home run.

"Yahooooo!" he screamed.

"Atta baby, Mitchell!"

"Outta sight! Absolutely outta sight!"

When Scrapper reached home all of his teammates had surrounded the plate and were waiting for him. They lifted him up on their
shoulders and carried him back to the dugout.

The air was filled with cheers, horns, and
confetti. At 9-0, the game was history. About an
hour later, the American League Championship Series was all tied up at one game apiece.

ELEVEN

Roberto watched his team play the next two day games in St. Louis from the bench. At night, he watched the Boston-Chicago battles on TV in his hotel room. It was frustrating, nerve-racking, and irritating, but there wasn't anything else he could do.

Game three in the National League was a squeaker. St. Louis fell behind by one, rallied back to tie it up, fell behind again and rallied back to tie, and then, finally, scored in the bottom of the ninth to win, 3-2.

With their backs to the wall, the Dodgers came back and won game four. They finally showed some offense and put up four runs in the first. They went on to win 6-3 to even the series at two games apiece.

With retirements and injuries wrecking the Dodgers' usual set pitching rotation, Roberto was unsure where he would fit in again. During the 162 game regular schedule, L.A. pitchers would normally go every fifth day. Once the play offs started, the manager intended on using his best pitchers every fourth day.

Roberto's success at the end of the season had earned him consideration as one of the best pitchers. Magic knew he would pitch game seven — if there was a game seven.

"Hey, Magic," Steve Henderson called out to his teammate while getting ready for game five. "Whadya think of last night's game?"

Roberto continued to button up his jersey as he sat in the Dodgers' locker room. He turned to face his battery mate and shook his head. "Heckuva game. I couldn't believe Boston pulled it out again. Chicago's gotta find a way to score some runs!"

"No kidding. They're not gonna win any defensive struggles with Boston. Those guys are just too strong."

"There really hasn't been a close game since their opener. Chicago won the second game nine-zip, and now Boston's come back at home with seven-to-three and eight-to-one wins. It could go either way."

"You can't worry about that. We've got enough problems getting to the Series ourselves. Besides, Mitchell and Green have played real well. If the rest of their teams can't get it together, nothing they can do about it."

"Yeah, well for Mitchell it's all or nothing. It doesn't matter that he's doing the job. He's gonna feel responsible for not getting everyone else to perform."

Henderson shook his head. "Yeah, well, like I said, there's not a whole lot you can do as a second baseman to stop those home runs flying over your head. Boston's just got too much fire-power."

Roberto grew silent. He wondered if that was what they were gonna say if he had to face them.

A voice boomed out from behind the row of oak lockers. "Ramirez, in my office."

"Oh oh!" Magic said, cringing. "What did I do wrong now?"

"Don't be so paranoid," Henderson told him. "He's probably gonna tell ya you're throwing when we get back to L.A."

Roberto blinked and trotted toward the manager's office. In a moment he was back at his locker.

"Well?" Henderson asked.

"You were right! I'm going to pitch game seven!"

"All right. You stick with me kid, and we'll pull this out yet. Then, it's on to the World Series!"

David stepped out onto the field at Fenway Park and quickly scanned the stands. "Not an empty seat in the house," he said, smiling.

His eyes continued upward to the roof. As was his habit, he checked which way the wind was blowing from each corner of the stadium. Another smile creased his face. It was blowing out over the Green Monster.

With a three-game-to-one lead in the American League Championship Series, all the Boston players were relaxed and happy, eager to wrap it up. After splitting two games in Chicago, Boston had proven to be unbeatable at home — just as David had told Glen they would be. Their major concern was where to hold their victory party. David was sure it was going to be a blast.

Racing out to his position in center, the former Rosemont Rocket took a deep breath and soaked in the emotion charged air. He knew this was the game. Chicago wouldn't leave anything in the bag in this one.

Glen was the second batter up in the top of the first. Batting .560 in the series and leading his team with six RBIs, he was on a tear. Boston pitchers had tried everything but couldn't find the winning combination. Inside, outside, high, or low — if it was in the strike zone Scrapper was hitting it. On the first pitch he jumped all over a curve ball and smashed it to left field. Before it could be retrieved, he stood on second with his third double of the Series.

David shook his head in admiration. "Damn, he's ripping that ball!"

But as happened all too often in the series, the rest of the White Sox couldn't deliver and Mitchell was left stranded. Relieved, David ran into the dugout and started pumping up his teammates.

"Okay, guys, let's get to 'em early. Knock 'em out quick before they get anything going."

His teammates slapped high-fives. Everyone was psyched for this game.

But Chicago had different ideas. Mark Jackson, the powerful left-hander for the White Sox, was pumped up himself. His fastball was a blur as the first two Boston players struck out with their bats on their shoulders.

DT strode to the plate.

"Let's go, guy. You can do it. C'mon!" his fellow players yelled.

David was batting .490 in the Series and had nine RBIs. There was no question that he stood to be series MVP if Boston won. His power had won two of the games outright, and his timely hitting helped in the other Red Sox win. Those players who had been worried when Ross went down with an injury had already forgotten their fears. David had been simply awesome since assuming the starting role.

Jackson started David off with a fastball on the outside of the plate. It just hit the corner and the umpire called it a strike.

The Chisox hurler whipped his left arm in and let fly with another fastball — only this one was not outside. At the last possible millisecond, David spun around and dove to the ground. The ball whizzed by the bill of his batting helmet.

Jumping up, David took a quick run toward the mound, his bat cocked in his hand like a club. Before he could get there, every player from both teams was on the field. The play-off pressure had put everyone on edge. The bean-ball lit the fuse.

"Okay, smartass, let's see what you've got!" David screamed at the pitcher as he reached the dirt circle.

After the catcher tackled David from behind, a huge pig pile formed as player after player jumped into the mayhem. Before order could be restored, a dozen separate little skirmishes had started and been broken up.

"All right, all right. Everyone back in their dugouts," the head umpire screamed. "I'll sort this out."

Meeting with his other officials, he decided not to throw anyone out of the game. Instead they gave stern warnings to Jackson, his manager, and Boston's manager to keep everything under control. When they received those assurances, they signaled for the game to resume.

David dug in at the plate and waited.

"C'mon, wimp, put it over the plate!" he yelled out to the mound.

"Cool it, Green," the umpire warned him. "I'm not gonna put up with any of that!"

Jackson looked over to the dugout and got a quick set of signals to walk this batter. He nodded and delivered three pitches, all well out-

side. Now David was on first. The next batter
struck out and the first inning ended, 0-0.

The next five innings turned into a defensive
struggle — just what Chicago wanted. Staying
in striking distance was important for its offense.

Glen came up in the top of the seventh with
the score still knotted at zero. Again he took
the first pitch he saw and smacked it into left
field, this time for a single.

Without a moment's hesitation, he took off
for second on the first pitch to the next batter.
His jump off the pitcher was so good that he
slid in for a stolen base without even drawing a
throw.

"Okay, Robertson, deliver me. Now's the
time," Scrapper called out to his teammate.

Edging off the bag as far as he dared, Glen
tried to distract the Boston pitcher. He made
several bluffs as if he were about to run toward
third. Finally, the pitcher had to step off the
mound and look him back to the bag.

"Wayda go, Scraps," his teammates cheered.
"He's confused out there. You've got him."

Sure enough, when Ellis finally delivered his
pitch to the plate the Chicago left fielder
rapped it into right field for a single.

Racing around third, Scrapper tore for the
plate, dove, and just beat the throw. Chicago
was ahead, 1-0. The score remained 1-0 until
the bottom of the eighth.

Boston had been unable to touch Reed, and it looked to all the Red Sox fans as if the Series were heading back to Chicago.

After the first batter popped out to the catcher, Dave Myers drew a walk. The fans got back into the game and started clapping for a rally. When the next batter struck out they grew quiet again.

David stepped into the on-deck circle and waited. He hoped that somehow he could get up to bat with runners on. "We need something big right now," he said as he took his practice swings.

Frankie Statler, Boston's first baseman, took two strikes before stepping out of the box. David could see the sweat dripping down the side of his face. Stepping back in, Statler chopped at the next pitch and sent a dribbler down the third base line. The Chicago fielder barehanded it and threw to first. Statler beat the throw.

"All right!" David yelled.

The fans rose to their feet. They could smell blood and were hungry for the knockout. Screaming now, they pleaded with David to deliver the fatal blow.

Scrapper paced around at second. The pit of his stomach was rolling over and over and his lips were dry and cracked. He wanted the win so badly he could hardly stand it. The tension was eating him alive.

David dug his cleats into the batter's box and cocked his bat backward. He noticed his left elbow shaking as he tried to hold the bat upright. He didn't realize how keyed up he was. Holding up his right hand, he called time and stepped back out of the box.

Taking a couple of deep breaths, he shook his head to clear the cobwebs and focused his eyes on the Chicago pitcher.

"Relax. You can do it," he told himself over and over again.

The crowd was on its feet now. The roar from the stands was like a thousand airplanes revving up their jet engines. The players could no longer hear anything else and flashed hand signs to each other to communicate.

Glen motioned for the outfielders to move farther back. Already near the warning tracks, they, like everyone else, knew what David's game plan was going to be.

The first pitch, a hard slider moving away from him, was all David needed. Nearly jumping out of his shoes, he put every fiber of his body into the swing and caught the ball just as it reached the front of the plate. Dead on.

Though seemingly impossible, the noise in Fenway got louder. There was no doubt in anybody's mind where the ball was headed.

David went into his best home run trot. His teammates jumped up and down, tossing their hats and cheering. The air was filled with confetti, programs, toilet-paper rolls, seat cushions, and cups.

When he finally hit the plate David heard a loud explosion of fireworks and looked out at the scoreboard. Boston had the lead 3-1. All 37,000 fans and 25 Boston players knew who was going to win. Most of the Chicago players did too.

When the next Boston batter flew out to end the inning the team was given a standing ovation as it took the field. They were only three outs away from the American League pennant.

Chicago's first batter grounded out, and the crowd got back on its feet, cheering each pitch.

Glen sat in the White Sox dugout and stared out. He wanted only one more chance. Glancing at the lineup sheet at the end of his dugout, he saw that he was behind four more batters. It didn't look as though he would get up again. But then the next batter beat out an infield single, and the next tapped a clean single up the middle. And suddenly, Chicago was in a last-ditch rally.

Ellis, the Boston pitcher, was clearly worried. Afraid of giving up another hit, he walked the next batter, and all of a sudden the bases were loaded.

Glen entered the on-deck circle. "C'mon, Rick, you can do it," he hollered at his shortstop.

Joe Morgan came out of the Boston dugout. He signaled for his ace reliever, Rex Caldwell.

While he was taking his warm-up pitches, Scrapper nervously walked back and forth to his dugout.

"Just let me at him," he muttered over and over again. "I want him!"

When Caldwell finally took his sign the crowd started cheering again. "Get him outta there. Strike him out. Fan him!"

The score was still 3-1, Boston. The bases were loaded with only one out. Chicago's best hitter was due up next. The momentum was shifting dangerously back toward the White Sox.

Caldwell worked from the stretch and delivered. Finnigan jumped all over the pitch. He hit a sharp grounder to the left side. After a quick pickup, a flip to second, and a relay to first the stunned crowd started to realize what happened.

"Double play! It's over!" David yelled. "We won! We won!"

David leaped into the air and ran in toward his teammates. A mob scene developed out on the field. The fans tried to overrun the field, but security guards held them off. Instead they watched their heroes celebrating the victory in a giant pile of bodies out on the mound.

Glen was shocked. He watched the celebration for a second and then slowly walked back to his dugout. As the White Sox somberly drifted back to their clubhouse, Scrapper put his arm around his disconsolate teammate.

"Good try, Rick," he said. "It wasn't your fault. We all went out today at some point. You just got lucky and were the last one. We'll get 'em next year."

"Thanks, Mitchell. For a pain-in-the-butt rookie, you're all right."

TWELVE

Game six of the National League Championship Series was a nail-biter. Faced with elimination if they lost, the Dodgers were tentative and uptight going into the game. Roberto sat on the bench, his stomach in knots, wondering if he was going to get a chance to pitch in game seven.

In a game punctuated with sporadic hitting but sensational fielding, the score was still tied after six innings at 1-1. The fans rose for the seventh-inning stretch and attempted to stir up their lethargic team. Clapping their hands and stomping their feet, they tried to provide the spark that was obviously missing.

"C'mon you guys. Let's fire up out there," team captain Ron Feffer yelled to his team mates. "We're playing like we're trying not to lose instead of trying to win. Let's show what we're made of!"

He got no response. The rest of the team just looked out onto the field.

Roberto couldn't speak for anyone else, but he knew he was so nervous it was hard for him to talk. His mouth was dry and his hands were sweating from the pressure.

When the Dodgers were retired in order in the bottom of the seventh, team morale was low. St. Louis's first batter smacked a single to center and every head out in the field drooped.

But the Dodgers were at home and the fans refused to let their team fold up. The organist started a familiar refrain, and the crowd started screaming, "Defense . . . Defense . . . Defense!"

The sound got louder and louder until the stadium started to rock and roll from the thundering cheers. The players felt the energy generated by their loyal supporters and concentrated on winning the game for them.

The next St. Louis batter hit a high hopper over the pitcher's head. What would have been a hit just a few minutes earlier now became the start of a fantastic double play. Shortstop Damon Smith made a leaping catch and flipped to second to catch the runner coming down. The relay to first was just in the nick of time.

The twin killing made the fans yell even louder. Pumped up by the support, the Dodgers' pitcher struck out the fourth batter to end the inning.

In that brief period in the top of the eighth the fans had managed to switch the momentum of the game — and the whole series — back to the Dodgers.

L.A. started the bottom half of the eighth with a single up the middle. The spark generated an explosion. Feffer followed with a double off the wall in center. Mike Lambert's single which brought home both runners, was all they needed for the victory. A homerun by Henderson brought in two more runs and the sixth game was history. The Dodgers had evened up the series at three games apiece with the 5-1 victory.

The locker room after the game was near bedlam. Everyone on the team knew that game seven was going to be theirs.

Everyone, that is, except Ramirez.

Sitting at his locker, alone and away from the noise of his teammates, Magic knew what was expected of him. "Starting pitcher . . . game seven of the NLCS. I hope I can handle it," he said to himself as he pulled off his uniform top.

The traffic jams on the drive to Dodger Stadium for game seven of the NLCS the next day didn't register in Roberto's head. He was in a complete daze. In a few minutes he was going to pitch the most important game of his life. A game that would give him and his teammates a chance to play against the Boston Red Sox . . .

and his old teammate David Green . . . if they won.

After dressing for the game in silence Roberto put his watch on top of the pile of clothes inside his locker and shut it. Tugging on his royal blue cap with the white tackle twill "LA" on the front, he grabbed his glove and headed out of the locker room for the field.

The Thursday evening crowd was arriving late as they fought the heavy Los Angeles commuter traffic. Roberto warmed up out in the bullpen while the stands continued to fill.

He had watched his two high school buddies battle it out in Boston on TV over the weekend. He was happy for DT and glad he wasn't around Scrapper after the White Sox lost. He was the worst loser around.

When the first St. Louis batter finally stepped up to the plate Roberto took several deep breaths and looked in for the sign. He could feel his heart thumping in his chest and struggled to control the pounding he heard in his head.

Steve Henderson, the Dodgers catcher, knew that his pitcher would be a bundle of nerves. That was one reason he called a simple fastball for the first pitch, and set up with a big target right down the middle of the plate. He wanted Magic to get off throwing strikes. A bad start could spell big trouble for the rookie right-hander.

The infield didn't help either.

"You can do it, Magic!"

"Let 'er rip, Ramirez!"

"Hum it in there. Hum it in there!"

Winding up, Roberto nearly closed his eyes as he started the pitch. He felt as if his stomach were filled with battery acid trying to burn its way to the surface. Sweat poured from his forehead, and it wasn't from the heat.

When the pitch pounded into Henderson's glove and the umpire yelled, "Strike one!" a tremendous weight was lifted from Roberto's shoulders.

"All right," Roberto said out loud.

Relieved, Henderson asked for the curve ball. When it broke down sharply and hit the outside corner of the plate for another strike, he flipped his rookie pitcher a thumbs-up sign.

The split-fingered fastball was next and Magic had his first strikeout. The Dodgers crowd went crazy.

After two more quick strikeouts the L.A. players were running back to the dugout, anxious to get their first at bats.

"Good job, Ramirez," Feffer told the rookie as they sat down in the dugout.

"Thanks, man. I was a little nervous out there."

Feffer laughed. "Yeah, who isn't, kid? But we're gonna ace this game and you got us going strong."

But the Dodgers couldn't get anything going in the first. After Magic struck out the side in the second, they felt like they were in control.

The tension and excitement of the game had made Roberto oblivious to an amazing fact. When he struck out the first batter in the Cardinals' half of the third, it was his seventh straight K.

The public-address announcer came on and said, "Ladies and gentlemen, Roberto Ramirez has just set a new LCS play-off record by pitching his seventh consecutive strikeout!"

The crowd erupted in cheers as it rose to its feet. Trying not to lose his concentration, Roberto quickly doffed his cap and resumed his position on the rubber. The fans continued to cheer even when he started his windup and the next pitch.

On a two and two count, the Cardinals' Brian Todd broke the spell with a single into left field for their first hit.

After that, things settled down to normal. Roberto continued to pitch a terrific game, but the Dodgers still failed to mount an offense of their own. Their only real threat was in the fifth. A lead-off walk was followed by a single to put runners on first and third. But a brilliant pick-off move by St. Louis starter Ronnie Davis caught the runner at third. A double play followed and the inning was over. After seven complete innings the score was still 0-0.

When he took the mound to start the eighth,
Roberto fired in a couple of warm up tosses and
stopped. For the first time in his life, he felt
tired out on the mound. He took a deep breath
and started rubbing the baseball between his
fingers.

Digging deep for whatever reserve was left,
Roberto let fly with his first pitch. It cut across
the plate waist-high for a strike. Two more
split-fingered fastballs and the first Cardinals
batter was retired. The next two batters
bounced out on first pitches, and the St. Louis
half of the inning was over.

Relieved, Roberto wiped the sweat from his
brow and glanced out at the scoreboard. The
string of zeros was long and straight:

000 000 00-0 4 0

000 000 00-0 5 0

As had been their custom throughout the series, the eighth proved to be the launching pad
for the Dodgers hitters. With the crowd cheering their encouragement, they started to do
some serious hitting.

A single by Reese started off the uprising. He
took a cautious lead off first, wary of Davis'
pick-off move. The crowd roared, hoping to get
the go-ahead run across.

Reese took a walking lead off the bag, and
before he knew what had hit him the throw

was coming over from Davis. Diving headfirst, he just made it back in time.

"Hey, Reese, watch it," the first-base coach cautioned.

"Came out of nowhere, Coach," Reese grumbled.

Feffer was up next. He carefully worked the count to three and two. On the payoff pitch, he slammed a long fly ball out toward the center field wall. The crowd rose to its feet in anticipation of a home run.

But the St. Louis center fielder raced back to the warning track and made an incredible leaping grab up against the wall to snag the long fly.

The crowd groaned in agony as Reese trotted back to first. When the next batter walked, though, the lineup came to life. Now, with a runner at second, it would take only a single to get a run in.

The St. Louis manager went out to the mound. Worried that his ace was starting to tire, he conferred with the catcher before deciding to stay with him.

Davis worked the ball over, rubbing it with his hands, while the manager walked back to the dugout. When Toby Harris, the Dodgers first baseman, stepped up to the plate, Davis was ready to go.

His first pitch to Harris tied him up in knots and produced a slow dribbler back to the mound. Davis fielded it cleanly and fired the ball to third for a force-out. The other runners managed to beat the relay throws and were safe.

Now there were two outs, and there were still runners on first and second. It just didn't seem that L.A. could get that runner around and in.

Henderson lumbered to the plate next, hoping that he could get on base. He smiled when he heard his battery mate calling from the dugout.

"C'mon, Henderson," Magic yelled. "It's up to you, man." Henderson tipped his batting helmet in the direction of the dugout and dug in at the plate. The fans continued to buzz in anticipation of a hit. They knew their team needed one now desperately.

The first pitch was a blazing fastball for a strike. Henderson never got the bat off his shoulder.

"Be a hitter up there," someone in the stands yelled out.

Davis, working from the stretch to hold the runners close, looked in for the sign and started his next delivery. The curve ball started out right over the middle of the plate about waist-high but didn't break. Henderson teed off on the lame-duck pitch and drove it with all his power.

The crowd jumped to its, feet and all the Dodgers ran up the first step of the dugout to watch the flight of the long hit. Dodger stadium exploded in cheers when the ball finally came down in the aisleway, twenty rows up from the wall.

Three runs came dancing in across the plate as the team formed a reception line at home. Waving and jumping up and down as they headed for the dugout, the whole team knew the game was theirs. Henderson punched the air with his fist after his dramatic home run, and the first player to greet him was Magic.

"Wayda go, Stever. I knew you could do it!"

Henderson slugged him in the shoulder. "Hey, now you can relax."

When the Cardinals came up in the top of the ninth, it was no contest against Magic's pitching.

The first St. Louis batter chased a split-fingered fastball for a strikeout. Batter number two hit a two-hopper back to the mound, which Roberto fielded and pegged to first for the out. With the fans roaring on every pitch, Magic bore down on the final hitter and let fly with everything he had. The man swung at the first two pitches for strikes. The third he never even saw.

"Strike three!" screamed the umpire, and Dodger Stadium went berserk.

The final strikeout gave Roberto two more LCS records: most strikeouts in an LCS game (seventeen), and highest leap from the mound for a winning pitcher!

"Yahooooo!" he screamed after the final out. "We did it!" The team mobbed him and carried him off the field on their shoulders.

The wild victory celebration started in the Dodgers' clubhouse. Television crews and commentators scrambled for interviews. Champagne bottles popped open, and bubbly spirits were poured over everyone in reach.

Before the party had got completely out of hand the voice of the Dodgers' clubhouse attendant called out over the raucous noise, "Hey, Magic . . . telephone."

"Tell him I'm drowning in champagne, man!" Magic called back as Feffer soaked his head for the second time.

"Okay, but it's long distance."

"No, wait," Roberto said, wiping his face. "I'll get it."

Must be my folks, he thought as he struggled through the mass of bodies hollering and throwing things around.

"Hello," he screamed into the mouthpiece over the noise.

A deep, gravelly voice growled through the receiver, "I'm coming to get you, Ramirez!"

"Who is this?" Magic said, laughing. "Speak up a little so I can hear you!"

"I'm you're worst nightmare," the voice said. "Worse than an A-ball bus trip."

Magic finally recognized the voice. "DT! Hey, what's going on?"

"Nothing, except we're both playing in The World Series!"

"Yeah, listen to this." Roberto held the phone out into the locker room party so DT could hear the noise. "We're celebrating toasting you guys already."

"Enjoy it while you can," David said. "In a couple of days it's gonna be nothing but misery and suffering."

"No way, man. We've got the *magic* to kick—"

Someone grabbed the towel around Roberto's neck and started to run off with it. Holding the receiver with one hand he snatched it back before the bandit could get away. He turned his attention back to his friend.

"Yeah, right. Seven games against the Cardinals. C'mon, we would've blown those chumps out in four straight. Look what we did to Scrapper's team."

"Pure luck. How'd he take it anyway?"

"You can ask him yourself when you see him at the games."

"What!" Magic yelled into the receiver.

"Ramirez, listen to me. He's gonna be at all the games."

"But how—" Henderson doused him with another bottle of champagne. He snapped his soaking towel at the catcher, then wiped off. "Sorry, man, things are getting wilder every minute here. Did Scrapper get his old man to spring for the tickets or what?"

"Get real . . . " David grumbled. "Scraps talked himself into a part-time job as guest commentator for the *Rosemont Register* for the World Series games."

"Whoa, that sounds great! The old hometown paper's going big time, huh?"

"You know it."

"So, what's the game plan? When am I gonna see you guys?"

"Hey, dummy. You tell us," David said. "You're the one who's coming over here to Boston. When are you guys supposed to get in?"

"Gimme a break, Green. We haven't had any time to talk about that stuff yet."

David laughed. He heard the loud commotion in the background and knew what his friend was talking about. "Okay, Magic. You go back and celebrate. It'll be your last one of the season."

"We'll see about that, smartmouth. Good pitching always stops good hitting."

"And *great* hitting always beats good pitching."

"Keep dreaming, Green. It's good for you."

DT continued. "Okay, guy. Party, have fun, pack your bags, and get ready . . . "

"For?"

"The Rosemont Rockets' reunion at the World Series!"

Tensions run high when DT Green plays against his best friend, Magic Ramirez, as the Boston Red Sox and Los Angeles Dodgers battle for World Series championship in . . .

6: SERIES SHOWDOWN.

INTRODUCING

★HEROES★
INC

EXCITING NEW SERIES
THAT ARE ADVENTURES IN
IMAGINATION!

BLITZ